THE STONEBRIDGE MYSTERIES

-5-

MISTLETOE AND CRIME

CHRIS MCDONALD

RED DOG
UK

Hardback ISBN 978-1-914480-88-1
Paperback ISBN 978-1-914480-09-6
Ebook ISBN 978-1-914480-51-5

www.reddogpress.co.uk

MORE IN THE SERIES

The Curious Dispatch of Daniel Costello

Dead in the Water

Meat is Murder

The Case of the Missing Firefly

1

CHRISTMAS LIGHTS

THE CREDITS ROLLED on the Rom-Com Helena had chosen and, as the lights in the cinema grew brighter, she looked over at Adam. He had been reluctant to spend an evening watching good-looking actors saying cheesy things to each other, before the inevitable happy ending and overplayed Christmas hit to finish it all off, but had agreed after much persuasion.

To his surprise, he'd enjoyed it. He even found that a single tear was rolling down his cheek.

'Are you crying?' she laughed.

'Crying?' he scoffed, wiping his face covertly with his sleeve. 'Of course not! It's just so bloody dusty in here and I think some of it got lodged in my eye. In fact, I'm going to have a word with management on the way out, see if they can sort the cleaners out.'

'Uh huh. Nothing to do with the kiss at the end?'

'God, no. I saw that coming from the opening scene. What a load of tosh.'

He grabbed his hoodie and bottle of water off the floor and noticed Helena try her best to hide a smirk. They walked hand in hand down the steps and through the foyer, where a crowd had gathered by the doors.

The forecasters had been threatening it for almost a week, but seemingly the weather gods hadn't been listening, instead keeping a hold of their festive payload until they decided the moment was right. Which was now, apparently. The clouds had unleashed their frozen cargo, covering the ground in a thick layer of fresh snow.

Suddenly, the doors of the cinema had been flung open and an impromptu snowball fight was underway. Adam and Helena watched as civilised moviegoers went to war, popping out from behind bins and running for cover behind walls. An older gentleman walked though no man's land, seemingly oblivious to the chaos erupting around him. A snowball, thrown from a fair distance, arced in the air and pasted the old man square in the forehead.

The crowd froze.

The old man stumbled backwards a couple of steps, and a young woman with a scarf pulled tight around her neck darted towards him. He held a hand up to her, bent down as if to pick something up, and stood again with a huge snowball in his hand.

'Who was it?' he shouted, and the crowd burst into laughter.

Adam and Helena made a run for it, taking only a few direct hits, before emerging into the relative safety of the town square.

The town hall looked stunning. Jonathan McClane, the mayor, had really gone all out this year. Fairy lights twinkled in every window, and neon signs showing dancing bells and shooting stars were attached to the ancient stone walls, spilling their colourful light onto the cobblestones below. An immaculately decorated Christmas tree took centre stage in the square; perhaps the biggest one in recent history.

'I see McClane got his way,' Helena said.

'It's *so* him to get his knickers in a twist about what colour baubles to use, isn't it? I mean, who cares if someone wants a bit of blue on it?'

'People like tradition at this time of year. I think the gold and red looks nice.'

He looked at her—her hair shining in the moon's gleam and the lights from the tree reflecting in her electric blue eyes, and he'd never felt more in love.

'You look nice,' he said.

'Shut up,' she replied, digging him in the ribs with a playful elbow.

She hooked her arm in his and they walked towards the car park. The snow still fell heavily.

'Let's take the short cut,' he said.

'Oh, not down Burnside Way. It always smells of wee.'

'But it's so much quicker and I'm freezing. Just hold your nose and you'll be grand.'

They quickened their pace slightly and slipped into the alley between Baldwin's, the town's department store, and a new outdoor sportswear shop. The walls were daubed with many years' worth of graffiti, mostly faded, but some areas had been topped up by today's would-be artists. Exit signs from the shops cast a green hue over the alley, illuminating something near the other end.

'What's that?' Adam asked, pointing.

'Bags of rubbish?' Helena suggested, squinting through the falling snowflakes.

When they reached the pile, they had their answer. Lying in the snow was a man, who might easily be confused for Father Christmas, were it not for his sullied clothes and unsightly appearance.

His trousers were filthy at the knees and his coat was light and completely useless for the current blizzard—though since he was dead, that didn't really matter.

The snow around his head was stained red, and blood still spilled from a nasty gash in his forehead.

Adam had to look away. He'd never been good with blood, and already felt lightheaded at what he'd seen. Luckily, Helena was a nurse at the local hospital, so slipped straight into professional mode. Before disturbing the scene in any way, she took her phone from her pocket and snapped a picture. She then checked for a pulse and performed CPR, while shouting at Adam to call for an ambulance.

It arrived not long after, though the poor man was pronounced dead at the scene. They called the police and in no time at all, DI Whitelaw strode up the alleyway towards them, looking annoyed that he'd presumably had to leave his comfy pyjamas and crackling fire behind.

'Well, well, well. It wouldn't be a crime scene without Adam Whyte sticking his beak in. I thought you'd given up on the detective work.'

'I didn't think you needed me anymore, now that you've bucked your ideas up.'

'We *never* needed you. It's been over a year since that nonsense on Winkle Island. What are you doing here?'

'We were walking back from the cinema and stumbled across him.'

'Who?'

'Gerald Agnew,' Adam said, pointing at the body. 'Surely you must know Gerald?'

'Course I know Gerald. Bloody nuisance,' Whitelaw said, casting his eye over the body.

Gerald Agnew was a Stonebridge institution. Homeless as long as Adam had been alive, he'd refused help from any of the organisations who had offered their assistance. Instead, he roamed the town like he owned the place. He was friendly in the day, as long as you threw him the odd quid as you passed, and a drunken pest at night.

'Well, at least this one is cut and dried. Looks like the old man tripped or slipped and smacked his head on that concrete bollard. From the looks of it, he either had a heart attack or his brain simply shut off. Of course, I'm not a medical expert.' Whitelaw shrugged. 'Unfortunate, but that's the way the chips fall sometimes.'

'What a lovely sentiment. Are you free to do the eulogy at his funeral?' Adam said.

'Button it, you, unless you want to spend the night in the cells.'

Adam held his hands up and Whitelaw disappeared out of the alley, leaving a young constable in charge of taking his and Helena's statements, though there wasn't much to tell. The young constable thanked them and left, shaking snow from his shoulders as he went.

Adam and Helena walked to a nearby coffee shop that was open late, hoping to entice late-night shoppers in with the promise of a bit of warmth. They slipped into a booth, ordered two hot chocolates and reflected on what just happened. She, matter-of-fact and stoic; he, still a bit light-headed from the sight of the blood.

They drank their drinks quickly, and then made their way back towards the car.

2

OLD HABITS DIE HARD

COLIN MADE HIS way around the lounge of the retirement home where he worked, clearing up the left-over bots of coloured card and doing what he could about the glitter that had fallen on the floor and started a new life within the plush, recently-laid carpet. Karen, the owner wasn't going to be happy, but at least the old folks had had fun designing their own Christmas cards. Most of them had gone off for an afternoon nap now, and Colin was glad of the peace and quiet.

He was almost finished when Barry came hobbling over. His health was going downhill rapidly, but he still had a mischievous glint in his eye.

'Son,' he said. 'What's happening with you?'

'Not a lot,' Colin replied, signalling to the mess of cardboard and paint. 'Clearing up after you messy pups.'

'Jesus. This is what I keep saying to you—you want to leave us old fogies behind and get yourself a job with a bit of excitement.'

'And what do I keep saying to you? Giving you a sponge bath is all the excitement I need in my life.'

'I used to live vicariously through you,' Barry said, pointing at Colin. 'Remember when there was that spate of crimes and you and your wee pal went and sorted them all? That was keeping me young. How long has it been?'

'Over a year, now.'

'A whole year since that trouble with the radio station yuppies? Goodness. No wonder I'm looking this old.'

'Are you still working your way through the Mackay series?'

'Aye, and they're great, don't get me wrong. But what you were dealing with in Stonebridge was real!'

Barry slinked off, fell into his armchair and was asleep within minutes. Colin continued his cleaning up and admitted to himself that he kind of missed snooping around too.

After a number of embarrassing blunders, there was an investigation into the Stonebridge police force, which resulted in them taking crimes in the town a bit more seriously. This meant that the kinds of miscarriages and oversights that Adam and he had looked into had reduced in number, rendering the amateur detective duo obsolete.

That, coupled with the fact that Adam and Helena's relationship was becoming more serious, meant that the erstwhile detectives weren't seeing a lot of each other at the moment—though their FIFA playing exploits had simply moved online.

Colin felt his phone vibrate in his pocket. When he pulled it out and checked the screen, he laughed.

'Your ears burning, were they?'

'What do you mean?' Adam asked.

'Never mind. What's up?'

'I was wondering if you were free for lunch? Be good to catch up.'

'I've got a break in about twenty minutes. Is that too soon?'

'No, that's perfect. See you at Ground?'

'Plan.'

ADAM WATCHED COLIN through the window, waiting for the green man to cross the road, despite the lack of traffic, like a small child. When the traffic lights finally turned red, he dallied across the road and in through the café's door. He appeared five minutes later, holding a tray, rammed with goodies.

'I didn't know if you had eaten already, so I got a McLaughlin special.'

Adam *had* already eaten a panini before Colin arrived, but still dove into the sweet treats with abandon. He was nervous, and the usually delicious doughnut made him feel a bit sick. He set it down, disappointed with himself.

'Everything okay?' Colin asked. 'Still cut up about the Gerald incident?'

'No. I'm grand. It's not like we've never seen a body before.'

'Yeah, but it's still pretty messed up. A corpse is not to be trifled with. Especially you, you know, with your disposition.'

'My what?'

'Your scaredy-cat nature.'

Adam shrugged, knowing that Colin had him bang to rights, and tried forcing another chunk of doughnut down his throat.

'What is it, if it's not the body? Are you dying?' Colin said. 'I've never seen you have to set a treat down before.'

'Fittest I've ever been. Have you seen my guns at the minute?'

'Seriously, dude. I've known you for twenty years. I know something's wrong.'

'I'm going to ask Helena to marry me,' Adam blurted out. 'I know we've not been together long, but it feels right, you know?'

There followed a stunned silence, before Colin leapt off his chair and enveloped Adam in a bear hug.

'This is massive, dude. Congratulations!'

'You're the only person I've told, so radio silence. I thought maybe we could go looking for rings today. If you want to.'

'Of course!'

'And, you'll be my best man, right?'

Tears sprung into Colin's eyes. Their friendship was a long one. They'd met on the first day of primary school and had been inseparable ever since. It was built on solid foundations—a mutual love of FIFA, Thai sweet chilli crisps and live music, and showed no signs of ending.

'Too right I will.'

They shook hands and chowed down on the treats, Adam's appetite returning with a vengeance now that he'd gotten his news off his chest, and his best friend's support.

'Why now?' Colin asked.

'Well, I just got a tax rebate for five hundred quid, and I figure if I don't buy a ring, I'll probably end up buying the new PlayStation instead.'

'Safer with a ring, I reckon.'

'Definitely.'

They finished up, cleared their tray, and headed down the narrow steps, emerging onto Stonebridge's high street.

'Tiffany's or Cartier, sir?' Colin laughed.

'I said five hundred, not five grand.'

'I reckon you'd even struggle with that. Winston's?'

'That's what I was thinking.'

They walked up the cobbled main street towards the town's more affordable jeweller. Charles Winston was a Stonebridge cornerstone. His shop had survived fires, break-ins and IRA bombs during the height of The Troubles, while changing a multitude of lives in the process, thanks to his sparkling diamonds.

A bell trilled above their heads as they walked in, and Adam immediately felt overwhelmed by the sheer number of diamonds, rubies and emeralds facing him.

Luckily, Charles was on hand.

The old man placed a bookmark carefully into the crease in the pages and slowly closed his novel. He pushed himself out of the leather armchair he'd been reclining in, and peered over the top of the counter, adjusting his fitted waistcoat in the process.

He looked, to Colin's eyes, like a little old tortoise. His wrinkled skin, wizened eyes and hairless head combined to give him a reptilian look.

'How may I help you today, young sir?' he asked.

'I'd like to buy an engagement ring.'

'Well, we can certainly help you with that.'

For the next twenty minutes, he ushered them this way and that. A ring would be placed in Adam's hand and snatched away almost immediately again, Charles grumbling about something or other.

'I can tell when someone loves one of the rings from the moment they set eyes on it,' he said, shuffling towards a display case with white gold banded rings. 'You haven't loved anything yet, but we'll find it.'

Colin excused himself and went outside, returning a few minutes later.

'What's up?' Adam asked.

'I've asked work to cover me a while longer. This is much more important.'

Charles handed Adam another ring, and took a step back.

'I think we've found the one,' he said.

And he was right. Adam had a feeling in the pit of his stomach that this was the ring he'd been waiting for. The silver band was thin, and a small, perfectly cut diamond protruded from the top. It was understated and quite beautiful.

'How much is it?' he asked.

'£450, but I'll knock twenty quid off so that the two of you can go and celebrate with a couple of beers.'

Adam paid the money and shook the kindly owner's hand, before placing the ring box in the inside pocket of his jacket.

As they left the shop, a man with lank hair spilling from beneath a soiled beanie hat strode up to them, like he'd been waiting for them to emerge.

'You're the two wee lads who like to play detective, aren't you?' he said, his voice slurred and stinking of cheap booze.

Adam tried to walk on, but the man grabbed his arm.

'I'm not making fun, or anything. I swear. I need your help.'

'What's wrong?' Colin asked.

'My mate was killed.'

'Gerald?'

'Aye.'

'I found the body,' Adam said. 'The police said he slipped and bashed his head off the pole.'

'Nonsense,' the man spat. 'Gerald was like a cat. Nine lives, man. And he'd got himself off the drink, too. Least, that's what he told us. There's no way he slipped.'

Adam and Colin cast a dubious glance at each other. Their new friend didn't notice. He was too busy throwing a can of cider down his throat.

'What do you think happened, then?' Colin asked.

'I was nearby. I heard him arguing with someone.'

'And?'

'It was heated. Serious stuff, by the sounds of it.'

'Do you know who it was?'

'I think so, but I'm no grass, man.'

Adam went to walk on.

'What are you doing?' the man asked.

'You're giving us nothing to go on, dude. You can't expect us to help you out, when you won't tell us what you know. You're wasting our time.'

'Alright, alright. It was Marty Hesketh.'

'Jesus.'

'Aye. Now you know why I wanted to keep my mouth shut. He and Gerald were arguing, quietly. Intense, you know what I mean? I didn't know who it was at first, and I was going to go down and sort it out, but then I recognised the voice, so I scarpered. I don't want to be on Marty's bad side.'

'And you're sure it was Marty?'

'Well, I'm not 100%. But I assumed as much. He likes a fight, does Marty, and him and Gerald were two of the same.'

'But you can't be sure?'

'No,' he said, shaking his head.

'So, you heard them arguing?'

'Aye, and I scarpered. Like I just said. Heard a scream from the alley and then I saw the police and the ambulance and all sorts piling in not long after. Reckon they'd come to sort it all out, and then I find out that Gerry's died and the police have done nothing about it.'

'Were you drunk at the time?' Colin asked.

'Pished as a newt, aye,' he nodded.

'And you think Marty killed him?'

'Aye.'

'So why not go to the police?'

'And tell them what I know?' he laughed. 'Aye, they're going to take the word of a tramp and reopen a case. That would mean them getting off their fat arses and actually doing some work.'

'Why us?' Colin asked.

'Because you two boys get stuff done. I've read about you in the papers. Yous are like Batman and Robin. Yous hear about an injustice and yous get to the bottom of it.'

Adam looked at Colin.

'We can't promise anything,' his friend said.

'You've made my day for even considering it. God bless yous,' he said, and sloped off towards the town hall.

'We can't promise anything?' Adam repeated.

'It's a kind way of saying no,' Colin shrugged. 'You were there. Did anything seem off to you?'

'I don't think so.'

'There we are then.' Colin looked at his watch and swore. 'I'm going to be late for work. Congratulations again, dude. Let's have a beer tonight to celebrate.'

Adam watched him rush off, slipping comically a few times on the watery slush that was slowly turning to ice. He walked back to Ground and ordered a hot chocolate, before taking a corner seat and thinking about how best to propose.

But he couldn't focus, and his mind wandered to Gerald's body.

Something had been nagging him since Colin had asked if anything was 'off' about the scene in the alleyway.

The blood and the body had combined to immobilise Adam's senses at the time—the horror of it all taking up too much space in his mind. But, with the benefit of hindsight, the little sixth sense in his brain was picking something up, but couldn't quite pinpoint what *it* was.

He pulled out his phone and texted Helena, asking her to send through the photo she'd taken of the alleyway. She replied almost instantly, and the contents of his hot chocolate nearly resurfaced.

He put his thumb over the image of the body—out of sight, out of mind—and concentrated instead on the surroundings. The lighting wasn't great, rendering the image dark and grainy, though the flash from the camera had helped a little.

He studied the background and honed in on what he'd missed when he was actually there.

Footprints in the snow.

Footprints leading away from the messy body.

Either someone had used the alleyway as a shortcut, seen the body and walked on past without telling a single soul. Or, whoever the footprints belonged to had murdered Gerald Agnew and strolled away without a second thought.

3

THE HARDEST MAN IN STONEBRIDGE

ADAM WAS JITTERY. Had been all day since he'd bought the precious goods.

He imagined that the little box containing the ring, lodged in his jacket pocket, was giving off some sort of homing beacon signal, and every time Helena's eyes drifted towards it, he'd asked her what she was looking at. It seems he'd snapped at her too many times.

'What is up with you today?' she sighed, as she lifted his plate and took it to the dishwasher.

'Nothing. Sorry. I'm just tired.'

'Well, for everyone's sake, go to bed early. I've got yoga soon, so I'm going to go and get ready.'

She touched his shoulder gently as she walked past him on her way to the bedroom, and he flinched, thinking she was going to shake him down to find out what he was hiding.

Thankfully, she didn't notice.

When he looked at his phone, he saw a message from Colin, asking if he was still on for the pub later.

Just for one pint, he typed, before pocketing his phone.

'I'M GOING TO have to propose soon,' he said, lifting the glass and clinking it against Colin's. 'I'm going out of my bloody mind. I'm fully convinced she's ex-Spetsnaz and that she knows exactly what I'm up to.'

'Spetsnaz?'

'Russian Secret Service.'

'You've been playing too much Call of Duty.'

'Maybe,' he agreed. 'I'm just so worried she's going to go into my pocket to look for change or whatever, and find it. I need to get it done.'

'Get it done. Ever the romantic.'

'You know what I mean,' Adam laughed, throwing a pack of nuts at his friend's face and catching him square in the forehead.

They sank back in their seats and enjoyed the fire crackling heartily in the hearth. Fairy lights twinkled and lush garlands ran along the bar top. The atmosphere in the pub was jovial and Elton John was blasting through the sound system, urging everyone to *Step into Christmas*. A few would-be karaoke singers were mouthing along while some Strictly wannabes were already shaking their moneymakers on the dancefloor.

On his phone, Adam accessed the picture of the alleyway and pushed it across the table. Colin took it and gave it a brief look.

'Flip me, there's a lot of blood. Looks like a still from a noir film. What am I looking for?'

'The footprints.'

'What about them?'

'The fact they're there, and they shouldn't be.'

'But you were there.'

'Yeah, but we came from the side of the alley that we're standing on. Neither Helena or me had been past the body when she took the photo.'

'So those footprints belong to someone else.'

'Ding ding ding! We have a winner.'

'And I'm assuming you're thinking that they belong to the killer?'

'Why else would they be there? No one is going to walk past a body and not do anything about it.'

'Maybe whoever they belong to went to get help? Or find a phone in a shop or something?'

'Yeah, maybe. But there's an invention now called the mobile phone, and most people have one.'

Colin ignored the sarcasm. 'So, what are you going to do?'

'I think I'll show the photo to the police, see what they think.'

'Good idea.' Colin passed the phone back across the table. 'Now, back to the proposal. What are you thinking? Something elaborate? Hot air balloon, or a dove carrying it to her or something like that?'

'Nothing tacky. Just something simple.'

'Probably for the best.'

'Do you want me to be there for morale support?'

'Thanks, mate, but I reckon I'll be okay.'

They laughed and touched glasses together again, and Adam was reminded once again how good of a friend Colin was to him.

THE NEXT DAY, Adam sat in the uncomfortable seat, squirming. A heater blasted the room with everything it had, causing sweat to crusade down his forehead and pool in his armpits. He wondered if the copper sitting opposite him was using these techniques to make Adam feel uneasy. If he was, it was working.

'And what's this supposed to be exactly?' DI Whitelaw asked.

'It's a photo of the alleyway when we found Gerald's body.'

'Bloody reporter now, are you? The bit of detective work on the side not enough for you?'

'My girlfriend took it. She's a nurse and thought it could be helpful down the line.'

'Good of her. You hired her for your agency yet?'

'Look, I know I've made you and your team look stupid in the past,' Adam snapped, unable to stop himself. 'I just thought you might be interested in potential evidence.'

'Evidence? Of what?'

'Murder.'

'Don't talk daft, lad. We were all there. Drunk as a skunk, he was. You could smell the fumes from Meadowfield. Took a tumble and bashed his head. It's unfortunate, but there's certainly no foul play here.'

'And what about the footprints?'

'All they show is that someone else was in the alley at some stage. All sorts of drunks and scallies hang around there.'

'But…'

'Listen to me,' Whitelaw said. 'There is no crime. Do you hear me? Don't go kicking that hornet's nest, 'cos all you'll get is a big old sting, and no one needs that around Christmas time, do they?'

'Always a pleasure,' Adam said, as he stood up and walked towards the door.

'Oh, and delete that photo, would you? It's voyeuristic and weird that you've got a snuff picture on your phone.'

'A snuff picture? So, you're saying he *was* murdered?' Adam replied.

'What?'

'A snuff movie is where someone is murdered on screen. Are you now saying he *was* killed, or are you just trying to sound cool?'

'I got my words wrong, alright?' He shrugged. 'Now, delete it or I'll have you chucked in the cells, no questions asked.'

Adam knew Whitelaw was blowing hot air, but couldn't resist winding him up a bit more. 'For what?'

'Wasting police time.'

Adam left the police station and called Colin, who answered immediately.

'How'd it go?'

'As expected,' Adam replied. 'DI Whitelaw was incredibly helpful and courteous and I have full faith in his ability to take the case forward. It's lovely to see that he has turned over a new leaf.'

'I can hear the sarcasm dripping from here.'

'He dismissed it without any questions. I think we should have a little nosey into it.'

'That means talking to Marty.'

'Yeah, true. But it does look suspicious.'

'Fine,' Colin sighed. 'As always, Adam Whyte is right.'

'That could be my campaign slogan if I ever ran for mayor.'

'What's the plan, then?'

'Shall I meet you at eight o'clock tonight at Wilson's?'

'Wilson's? Jesus, have you a death wish?'

'It's where Marty will be,' Adam said.

'Alright. If we have to. But you're buying the drinks.'

WILSON'S BAR WAS on the wrong side of town, near the vegan food stores and hippy clothing bazaars. If you were ever hankering for an illicit high, this was the pub for you.

Colin pushed the door open, imagining he was an out-of-towner barging his way into a foreign saloon. The décor hadn't been changed since the place had opened, and that had been some time in the 70s. No attempt had been made at making the bar look even a little bit Christmassy. Heads swung around and brows furrowed at this newcomer who they'd never set eyes on before.

Colin stared back and walked to the bar, Adam cowering behind him.

'Two pints of lager, please.'

The bar man set down the filthy rag he was wiping the bar top with and sighed pointedly, like pouring drinks was a huge inconvenience or outside his skillset. When they were done, he pushed the glasses towards them, spilling a good amount from each one. Colin looked at the spillage, and then at the bar man.

'Are we going to have a problem here?' the bar man asked.

'No problem. No problem at all,' Adam said. 'Thank you so much for your service.'

The bar man grunted and started to turn away.

'Is Marty in tonight?' Colin said.

'Might be. Who wants to know?'

'I want to know.'

'He's in the back room, at the table. I doubt he'd want to be disturbed.'

Adam and Colin ambled off, making a point not to thank him. Colin abhorred rudeness, so felt a little bit bad, but also felt like the bar man deserved it. They pushed through a door that led to a narrow corridor, walked past the toilets (which were letting out an unholy stench) and stood outside a door with a sign proclaiming it as the room designated for staff use only.

Colin knew this was a lie.

The Back Room was part of Stonebridge folklore. All sorts of illegal activities took place behind this famous faded door, if the stories were to be believed. Drugs, gambling, bare-knuckle boxing. Their late friend, Danny Costello, once claimed to have been in there when a cock fight happened, though no one believed him.

Faced with this door, even the usually unflappable Colin was feeling nervous. He raised a shaking hand and knocked lightly. Inside, the screech of a chair scraping across stone flooring sounded and a few seconds later the door opened an inch. A beady brown eye appeared.

'What?'

'Can we have a word with Marty,' Colin said.

The man replied with words unprintable here, and went to shut the door.

'We think he'll want to hear what we have to say,' Adam said, pushing his foot into the gap, so that the door couldn't close.

'He can be the judge of that,' the voice inside scoffed. 'Now, move your foot before I remove it with force.'

The eye disappeared and a minute later, the door was thrown open. Marty Hesketh was even bigger than Colin remembered him to be. His hair was a matted mess and his eyes were bright blue and wild. He was wearing a vest, despite the Wintery chill in the air, and had to turn sideways to get through the door. His arms were covered in tattoos that looked like a blind man had inked them.

'What?' he asked, closing the door behind him.

'We've heard rumours that the police are wanting to speak to you about Gerald Agnew's death. We're having a look into it too, and were wondering if you could answer a few questions?'

'A few questions about what? I didn't do nothing.'

Adam wanted to point out the double-negative, but also wanted to keep his face the way it was.

'Look,' said Colin. 'We know you weren't involved, but if you could answer a couple of our questions, we can help clear you. Officially.'

'Are you detectives?'

'We kind of are, yeah.'

The big man studied their faces for a minute.

'Oh, I know who you two are now. I've seen you in the papers. The two lads who keep making the police look like idiots. Aye, I'll talk to you, but only because I'm due a cigarette break. Let's go outside.'

They walked down the corridor, Marty following behind them like the boulder in Raiders of the Lost Ark. They pushed the back door open, which led them to a smoking area and beer garden, though the term garden was rather grandiose for what it was.

They stood under a sloping roof to protect them from the drizzle. Marty used a huge hand to shelter the cigarette from the wind while he lit it.

'Ask away, fellas. I've nothing to hide,' he said, blowing a lungful of smoke into the atmosphere.

'Did you see Gerald the night he died?'

'I believe I might've.'

'In the alley next to Baldwin's?'

'Yep.'

'Why?'

'Because, he'd nicked my spot. Everyone who's homeless knows that that doorway is the best in the town. The pipes from the shop next door give out a wee bit of warmth and Brownley's throw all its unsold food in the big bin outside.'

'And you wanted it back?'

'Too right I did. Gerald was a legend in town, but that was *my* spot. I couldn't believe it when I saw him lying in it with all his stuff.'

'What happened?'

'I pulled him up by his shirt and we had it out. Verbally, I might add, detectives.' He added the last word with a little wink, before carrying on. 'We came to an arrangement. He could have the spot for the night, and I could have some of his wares.'

'Wares?'

'Aye. Gerald had started dabbling in the world of drug dealing. I told him it was a stupid idea. Everyone knows that Stu has a monopoly on the area, and isn't shy about dealing with anyone who thinks they can muscle in on his patch.'

'And what did he say?'

'Told me he was making good money through it, and that he'd be off the streets before Stu even got wind of what he was doing. I told him that Stu probably already did know what he was doing, and that if I were him, I'd throw the rest of the drugs in the river and plead innocence.'

The thought of Marty Hesketh being afraid of anyone was almost humorous, but the myths and legends of Stu Finnegan's behaviour circled around Stonebridge like a cautionary tale. Even the police were afraid of him.

'You think Stu could've killed Gerald?' Adam asked.

'Mmhmm. And afterwards, he would've walked away without so much as a second thought. We done here?'

'One more question,' Adam said. 'Was it snowing when you spoke to Gerald?'

'No, it was sunny. Why?'

'No reason. Thanks for your time, dude.'

Adam held up a fist for Marty to bump. Marty looked at the fist, snorted derisorily at the gesture, and sauntered back to whatever unlawful activity awaited him in The Back Room.

'Smooth,' Colin said, as they left via the back gate.

4

THE SMILES

'HOW DO WE get our hands on some drugs, then?'

This was the question Adam posed to Colin, who looked at him with a furrowed brow.

'Not for consumption, obviously, but we need to talk to Stu, and buying the cheapest, least illegal drugs he has for sale is the obvious way in.'

'You want to break the law, just to try and see if Gerald was murdered? The police aren't arsed about the case, but if Whitelaw hears that we've been asking around and buying drugs in the process, you can bet he's going to take a sudden interest in you.'

'And who's going to grass us up? Stu?'

'Maybe someone will see us talking to him and put two and two together.'

'We've braved Marty Hesketh. I think we can take Mr. Finnegan.'

Colin sighed. He'd been dragged through enough nonsense in the past that had put his job—which he loved—in jeopardy. And now that he was manager, he had a lot more to lose. Still, Gerald starting to deal drugs and ending up dead not long after *was* suspicious.

'Look,' he said, at length, 'if we see him, we'll ask him about it. If not, it's no skin off my nose.'

'Grand,' Adam nodded. 'Are you heading to The Pacific tomorrow night?'

'Jeez, has it been another year already?'

THE SMILES WERE a mainstay of the North Coast's burgeoning music scene, and their annual Christmas gig was a time-honoured tradition. No matter where old friends had disappeared to—uni, jobs across the water or even further afield, years out, or emigration to the other side of the planet—the same faces always showed up for this event.

The Pacific was the chosen venue for this year's gig. It was a grotty dive bar with sticky floors and toilets that would have Ray Mears thinking twice about using them, but it had heart. You knew what you were getting when you turned up—warm beer and loud music—and that was enough to keep people coming back.

'No Helena tonight?' Colin asked, as Adam jumped into his car.

'Nah, she's been called in to A&E. Christmas, apparently, is a time when the general public drink too much and have too many accidents. Who knew?'

Colin drifted off from the kerb, and pressed a button on the dashboard, flooding the car with sixstarhotel's latest album.

'It's a crying shame that they've never hit the big time,' Adam shouted above the galloping bass and duelling guitars. 'Better than ninety percent of the nonsense in the charts.'

He quietened then, opting to play air drums for the rest of the journey. The Christmas gig always took him back to feeling seventeen again.

No responsibilities.

No worrying about bills or jobs or debt.

When the only stress in life was wondering why it was taking the girl you were texting so long to reply, and how many x's to put on the end of the message.

Colin pulled into a space that overlooked the ocean. The dark water looked to have swallowed a blanket of stars; the pinpricks of light pulsing off the calm surface. They got out and walked the short journey to the bar along the seafront, stopping to look at the huge mural that had recently been painted in tribute to a fallen comrade on the side of the building.

Inside, it was already sweaty. The windows were fogged with condensation and the air thick with sweat. Gunther, one of the support bands, were already playing, amps turned up to eleven and currently blasting through a punk rock version of *We Wish You A Merry Christmas*. A tentative mosh pit had started, while an elderly lady and her husband made their way to the nearest exit at speed, hands pressed firmly over their ears.

Adam and Colin watched the stage for a while, and when the band put down their instruments, made their way to the bar and ordered some drinks.

'Why aren't you drinking tonight?' Adam asked, as the bar man slid a pint in his direction.

'I've got my annual review tomorrow morning. I can't mark my first year as manager by turning up stinking of booze.'

'Fair point.'

Conversation was cut off as local heroes Split The Sky took to the stage. They'd disbanded years ago and reformed for a one-night-only affair, much to the delight of everyone in the room. The floor space was filled before a single note had been played, and the singer looked thrilled with the reception. He led the crowd in an acapella verse, before the instruments rushed in on a wail of feedback.

It was joyous.

Colin and Adam stood by the bar and soaked up every note. Friends they hadn't seen in a while congregated around them, though catching up was saved for when the band had finished.

When relative silence had descended again—after a number of encores that forced the band to play songs they'd already played once—stories of work, kids, and engagements were swapped and more drinks were bought.

While it was lovely to see everyone, Adam kept his eyes peeled for the arrival of Stu Finnegan. The plan was simple: ask for the smallest amount of drugs possible and while he was sorting it, probe him subtly for information. Once the transaction was complete, he'd flush the contraband down the nearest toilet.

A quarter of an hour later, Colin nudged Adam's arm and nodded his head towards the back of the room, for there stood Stonebridge's supplier of illegal goods.

'You actually doing this?' Colin asked.

'I'm actually doing this'.

He walked on shaky legs across the room, trying to look as natural as he could. The casual onlooker, if they'd caught Adam's approach out of the corner of their eye, might've described him as looking *too* laid back—like a caricatured version of The Fonz.

When he reached Stu, he stood nearby and tried to catch his eye. Stu smiled, spotting Adam's coy glances.

'We're not at a primary school dance, dude.'

'Ha!' Adam laughed. 'Good one. I'm just not sure how all of this works, you know?'

'What kind of thing are you after?'

'I don't know, really. I've got a tenner. What will that get me?'

'Little bag of weed.'

'Good,' Adam nodded. 'Yeah. A couple of spliffs will do just fine.'

Stu fished into his pocket and produced a small clear packet from it. Adam slipped him the ten pound note and took the goods, pocketing them before anyone could see what he was up to. Instead of walking away, Adam loitered.

'Can I help you with anything else, dude?' Stu asked.

'I hear there's a rival in town,' Adam said, raising his eyebrows conspiratorially.

'A rival? What are you on about?'

'Another dealer. Though, from what I hear, he won't be much trouble to you anymore.'

'Speak English, dude.'

'Someone else was selling drugs in town, but they were killed.'

'Ah, now you mention it, it rings a bell.' Stu scratched at a scab on his cheek, which was perhaps evidence of a recent scuffle. Adam wondered if this was a tell. If it was, he'd make a horrible poker player. 'It's a shame, but that's usually what happens to someone who tries to muscle their way onto my patch.'

'Really?' Adam whispered.

'No! Jesus! I don't go around whacking people because they're trying to take customers off me. People in this town know I get the good stuff, as you'll find out yourself soon. I take it you're a virgin?'

'I most certainly am not. As it happens, I've been with a couple of...'

'With drugs, I mean,' Stu interrupted.

'Oh, right. Yeah. In that case, yes, I am a virgin.'

'As I said, you'll see that my product speaks for itself. I don't need to go around battering people or intimidating them.'

'So you never spoke to Gerald?'

'Oh, we had words, but nothing physical. Trust me on that.'

His tone suggested that that was all he had to say on the matter. Adam thanked him for the drugs, hurried off to the toilet where he tipped the sweet-smelling cannabis into the filthy bowl and flushed it away forever. He washed his hands like Lady Macbeth, making sure none of the smell lingered on his skin, and finally re-joined his friends just in time for The Smiles.

He held off telling Colin what had happened, instead letting every other concern slip away as the music started. Looking around at the familiar faces as he let the folky goodness wash over him, he was gripped by a sudden melancholy. All of this— the camaraderie, old friends, the bands that he loved—all of this would one day come to an end, and it might never occur to them that *this* was the last time.

'I love you, dude,' Adam said to Colin.

'Don't be weird,' Colin replied, though he was smiling. He stretched an arm around his friend and pulled him close, before punching him playfully on the arm.

5

THE PROPOSAL

COLIN WAS SWEATING.

He hated formal meetings and he wasn't keen on suits and ties and buttoned-up shirts that felt like a boa constrictor had taken up residence around your neck.

The room felt like it was set up to intimidate, though they probably hadn't meant it that way. He sat in a hard, plastic chair facing three older, unsmiling gentlemen, whose suits looked like they cost a whole lot more than Colin's annual salary.

He pulled at his collar again, and answered their question about how he'd found his year as manager. He'd told them that it was a lot more responsibility, but that he had very much enjoyed it. He liked being in charge. He liked making sure the service users (he hated that word, but that's how the suits referred to the wonderful residents and he thought he'd keep it professional) had the best day they could possibly have.

The suits nodded along and then the head suit broke out into a wide smile. It was rather disconcerting.

'Mr McLaughlin, the service users here are very fond of you. We conducted a number of interviews prior to our meeting and they couldn't speak highly enough of you. A Mr, uh—' he checked his notes, 'McCullough...'

'Barry,' Colin interjected.

'Yes, Mr. McCullough was adamant that we should give you a pay rise.'

'That's nice of him.'

'So, Mr McLaughlin, how would you feel about continuing in the role?'

'Continuing?' Colin repeated. 'But I thought it was fixed term. Isn't Cindy coming back?'

'We're afraid not. Sadly, she's still unwell and has handed in her notice, which we have accepted. We were going to put an advertisement in the paper this week, but it seems you are the man for the job. If you'd like it, of course.'

Forgetting the norms of an interview, Colin jumped from his seat and shook each of the men's hands in turn, thanking them.

'I take that as a yes?' the lead interviewer asked, laughing.

'A huge one.'

WITH THE FORMALITIES completed, Colin drifted out of the room on a cloud and made a beeline for Barry, who he hugged. It wasn't a normal patient/carer moment, and Colin was sure Barry—a ninety-year-old man who'd fought in World War II—probably felt rather uncomfortable with the level of affection bestowed upon him. For now, Colin didn't care.

'What's all this in aid of, then?' Barry asked, when Colin had released him.

'You, you beautiful man, just secured my job for me.'

'I only said what I thought, son. If I thought you were a prick, I would've said that too.'

'And I appreciate it so much. You're a hero, and I get a bonus! Don't tell the others yet, though. Management want to do an announcement, you know?'

'Don't they know it's a retirement home? The news of your job is already out and forgotten about—Doris knew before you did!'

Colin patted him on the shoulder, and walked off to get him his tablets. When he returned with the small, white container full of colourful pills and a glass of water, Barry thanked him and then leaned in, conspiratorially.

'I've got an early Christmas present for you, young man.'

'Oh aye? PlayStation 5?'

'Ha! You should be so lucky. It's some information, about your case.'

He leaned closer still.

'It seems old Gerald was going up in the world before his untimely demise.'

'How do you mean?'

'Well, word has it that he was due to be the Santa in Baldwin's department store this year. He'd been for the fitting and everything.'

'But that's Tom Little's gig. Has been since I was a wee boy.'

'Twenty-four years,' Barry agreed. 'Would've been the big twenty-five this year. I don't know what Baldwin was thinking, but that's the word on the street.'

'The street?'

'Doris,' Barry said, nodding his head at the old lady in the corner with the purple rinse and the mouth moving at a hundred miles a minute. 'Nothing gets past old Doris.'

'Did she say anything else?'

'Plenty. But I can only just take in the headlines before I lose interest. Might be worth having a chat with Baldwin, if you can. He must have his reasons. Maybe something he says will shake a bit of information loose?'

'Good man, Barry. I'll see what I can uncover.'

'And while you're at the store, a nice bottle of brandy wouldn't go amiss for your helpful pal!' Barry shouted after the retreating Colin.

ADAM WAS ON one knee in the bedroom, looking in the mirror with the ring held aloft.

He'd always imagined proposing under the moon and stars, a picnic blanket laid out with a bottle of champagne waiting, but that was never going to happen in Northern Ireland. If he managed to find a moment when it wasn't raining, the constant wind rattling in off the sea would blow the picnic away, so Adam had resigned himself to doing it indoors.

Of course, asking the big question inside, in public, was also a no-go, in case of a negative response or a dog stealing the ring at the vital moment or some other unforeseeable incident. Best to do it in the confines of your own home, where other rooms were readily available to sulk in, if the answer wasn't what you wanted to hear.

He'd written a short speech on a piece of paper that was now damp with perspiration. It had curled at the sides and the ink was smudged, but Adam had read and re-read the words so many times that they were engrained in his head.

Now, all he needed to do was say them out loud and wait for an answer. One way or the other.

He puffed out his cheeks, slipped the ring box into his back pocket and walked out into the living room, where the unsuspecting Helena was lying on the sofa, half-watching Tipping Point and half dozing after her night shift.

Adam stopped suddenly.

He detested Tipping Point with every fibre of his being, and wondered if it being on television at the very moment he was going to pop the question was a bad omen.

'You okay?' Helena asked, peering over the sofa.

'Ah, yeah. I'm just going to get a drink. You want anything?'

'Ribena, please.'

Adam scurried away to the kitchen to regroup. He poured a drink but wasn't concentrating and it slopped over the side of the glass and all over the counter. Cursing, he grabbed a tea towel off the oven door's handle and wiped the spillage.

He couldn't think straight.

Bloody Ben Shepherd was living rent free in his head.

He took a few calming breaths, but could still hear the presenter talking kindly to the machine.

This wouldn't do. Maybe he'd wait until after the show, march in, turn the television off, get down on one knee and say his speech, and then show her the ring.

Yeah, that would do.

Having finished mopping up the puddle of lemonade, he threw the tea towel in the wash and returned to the living room.

'What's all the swearing about?' she asked, as she took her Ribena from him.

'Ah, spilled a load.'

'Goodness, I thought from the words you were using, you'd discovered a body or something.'

'Nah, all good. How's she doing?' he asked, nodding at the TV.

'In line for a couple of grand, I reckon. Fumbled a few soap questions, but brought it back with some rugby knowledge.'

They watched the rest, Adam enjoying not a single moment of it. When the jackpot had been won and the credits began to roll, he turned the television off and turned to look at her.

'What's going on?' she asked.

'Helena,' he said, his voice betraying him. 'I know you and me haven't been going out *that* long, but...'

'Adam, you're being weird. Are you breaking up with me or something?'

'No, nothing like that,' he said. 'Just let me finish.'

He composed himself and as he opened his mouth, his phone (which he thought he'd put on silent) started to ring. He pulled it from his pocket and pressed the red button.

'Who was that?' she asked.

'Colin. I can speak to him later.'

'It might've been important.'

The phone rang again and Helena told him to answer it.

'But...' he started.

'I need a shower anyway. Talk to your friend.'

She got up from the sofa and walked to the bathroom, while an angry Adam put the phone to his ear.

'This better be bloody good,' he said through gritted teeth.

'Oh, it is,' answered Colin.

6

A LITTLE SLIP UP

ADAM WAS STILL feeling raw when he got into his car and wondered, not for the first time, whether running around town trying to solve a crime—if it was a crime at all—was a good idea.

He realised that perhaps the energy he had devoted to those other "cases" was because his life had been empty at the time. There'd been no real job, no relationship and he'd been living with his mother. The thought of solving a crime was exciting, but maybe it was only exciting when you had the time to do it and nothing to lose.

Now, here he was, trying to ask the most important question he'd ever ask anyone, and instead of being able to say it, he was being called away to question an old man who'd been snubbed for this year's department store Santa role.

He started the engine, and sat stewing while waiting for the blower to defrost the windscreen. When it finally worked its magic, he reversed carefully out of the space and made his way into town.

COLIN HUDDLED IN the corner booth of the coffee shop, trying to keep away from the cold wind whistling in through the automatic door that was almost exclusively open. One hand was wrapped around a steaming mug of hot chocolate and the other scrolled through pictures on his phone.

It felt strange, judging people solely on their looks and a few spartan lines about their lives, but such was the way with dating apps.

Things were looking up for Colin. He'd landed a managerial role in a job he cared deeply about, and he was living in a decent enough flat in a nice part of town. But, truth be told, he was lonely.

Since Adam had found Helena, he'd seen less of his friend. Which, of course, was natural. And he was happy for him, but sometimes he wished that after a long day at work, he could come home and lie on the sofa and tell his girlfriend about his day.

So, here he was, scrolling through photos of girls in the hope that one would catch his eye. A few had, already, and they'd exchanged some messages but the chat had quickly died out.

What he really wanted was to meet someone the old-fashioned way—technology free. He wanted someone to catch his eye across the bar, to bump into someone as they pushed through a door at the same time; the pile of papers she'd be carrying would scatter and they'd spend a few laughter filled moments collecting them, their hands brushing on the last sheet.

He'd told this to Adam once.

Adam, in return, had told him that if he'd knocked a load of important papers out of a girl's hands in real life, she'd call him a couple of choice names, refuse his help, and that'd be that.

He was probably right.

A breeze blew through the coffee shop again, and with it came an unhappy looking Adam.

'You alright?' Colin asked, as Adam took the seat opposite him.

'I was about to ask Helena to marry me when you phoned.'

'Ah, man. Sorry! You should've told me to do one!'

'It's okay,' Adam said, softening. 'It probably wasn't the best way to do it anyway. Ben Shepherd, you know?'

Colin didn't know.

'Having the ring in the house is making me feel uneasy, is all,' Adam continued. 'I just hate all the pussyfooting around.'

'I hear you. I really am sorry. If I'd known, I would never have called you.'

'It's fine, honestly. What have you got?'

'Barry found out that Tom Little isn't going to be the Baldwin's Santa this year?'

'What?' Adam was gobsmacked. 'But he's as close to the real thing as it's possible to get.'

'I know. And apparently it was going to be his twenty-fifth year.'

'A quarter of a century? A landmark! Have you spoken to him?'

'No, I thought we'd go and see him now.'

'You know where he lives?'

'No, but I know where he works.' Colin pointed across the street at the pound shop which had taken up the prestigious space once held by M&S.

'Stonebridge's Santa Claus to pound shop seasonal drone. What a fall from grace.'

'Right?'

'Does Barry know who was going to be the Baldwin's Santa this year?'

'I'll give you three guesses,' Colin said, as he grabbed his stuff and slid out of the booth.

THE STONEBRIDGE POUND shop was a depressing place to be at the best of times, but at Christmas it was like walking into the seventh circle of Hell itself. It was heaving with bodies; little old ladies who battered their way through the crowd with walking sticks, stressed-looking mothers with screaming children who wanted every toy they came across, and flustered, middle-aged men who were simply panic buying whatever they could get their hands on.

Adam and Colin fought through the sea of people, searching for old Tom.

They found him, trying to placate a woman whose face was as red as a tomato. Someone, apparently, had taken the last roll of Paw Patrol wrapping paper.

'We have Peppa Pig,' Tom said, holding up a roll to show her.

'And how is that going to help?' the woman shouted back. 'My kids only like Paw Patrol. It's the only thing they watch. So how is this Peppa Pig roll going to work?'

Tom apologised, despite not having done anything wrong, and when she sighed and turned her back, he raised a middle finger in her direction. He just about managed to get his hand to his nose, turning the rude salute into a passable impression of a scratch. She gave him the evil eye and made her way towards the exit.

Tom picked up a pile of mince pie boxes and started to stack the depleted shelves.

'Mr Little,' Adam said, approaching him through the crowd. 'Would it be possible to have a few minutes of your time?'

'I'm a bit busy,' he said, looking over his shoulder. 'What can I help you with?'

'We have a few questions we'd like you to answer.'

'I'm behind schedule here. Can you tell me what you're looking for and I can guide you to an aisle?'

'It's about Gerald Agnew.'

He dropped the mince pie boxes at the mention of the name, and turned to give the boys his full attention.

'I've got a break in about twenty minutes. It's a short one, mind. Meet me out the front.'

HE EMERGED TWENTY-FIVE minutes later, his blue shop vest replaced with a heavy overcoat. His thick, white hair was combed to the side and his bushy beard bobbed with each step he took. He nodded curtly at them and led them to a side street, where he pulled a cigarette packet out of his pocket and lit up.

Watching the only Father Christmas you've ever known inhale from the toxic stick was an odd sensation, and a little bit of Adam's childhood died with the flicker of the lighter.

'Shame about poor Gerald,' Tom said. 'He was an annoyance round town, always asking for money and that, but freezing to death is no way to go.'

'He didn't freeze to death,' Adam said. 'He was killed.'

Tom looked sceptical.

'That's not what it said in the paper. Anyway,' he glanced at his watch, 'I know the two of you—what you get up to. What's this got to do with me?'

'How did it feel being canned from the Santa gig?' Colin said.

'Canned? God, you boys watch too much American TV. Look, I'd had a good run at it.'

'But you expected it to be you again this year, right?'

'Well, I assumed I'd be picked again, yes. Baldwin was making all the right noises, but in the end, he chose Gerald.'

'And how did you feel about that?'

'What do you want me to say?' He laughed. 'I was annoyed, naturally.'

'Decent money being Santa,' Colin said.

'Not to mention the kudos,' Adam added. 'Making loads of kids happy. To go from that, to having to deal with the likes of that woman who treated you like a slug on the bottom of her shoe. That must sting.'

'I know what you're trying to get me to say, but you don't know the half of it.'

'You must've been angry.'

'Yeah, alright, I was angry. Happy? How would you have felt? You're the king of Christmas for all those years and now you're having to stack shelves for hours on end, at my age. I was angry, alright? But not with Gerald.'

'Baldwin?'

Tom nodded. 'I always thought Kyle Baldwin was a stand-up guy. His father had been, so I thought his son would follow in the same mould. Sure, I'd heard the stories of how he treats some of his workers and stuff like that, but he was always dead on with me. And then I hear that he's gone and hired Gerald. Second hand. Didn't even have the cajones to tell me to my face. Got that bimbo secretary of his to do it for him.'

'So, what did you do?' Adam asked.

'What did I do? I did what every self-respecting Northern Irishman does when faced with a hardship—I went to the nearest pub and had a drink, bitched about it a lot and then I moved on.'

'And that's that?'

'That's that,' he nodded. 'Look, I know you two see yourselves as mini-Sherlocks. I've read the papers. You're good, better than that idiot Whitelaw. But I doubt there's a case here. Gerald was your classic drunk. If he didn't freeze to death, like the papers said, his liver probably gave up on him. It's no way to go, but it's not like it he didn't bring it on himself.'

'There's a Santa gig going now,' Colin said.

'Aye, he's been on the phone to me, ol' Kyle. I told him he could shove the Santa job up his…'

The end of the sentence was left unfinished, as Tom's manager chose the opportune moment to find him and remind him that break was over and his shift was due to start again.

Tom nodded at them, and told them that they were wasting their time. He wished them a Merry Christmas and then followed his boss back to work.

'I think if I'd actually heard Santa say the word "arse" then, it would've ruined my Christmas,' Colin said, as they left the side street.

7

BALDWIN

THE TOWN OF Stonebridge may well have been built around Baldwin's department store; such was its longstanding role in the community. The vast, red-brick building held the best plot in the town—you *had* to walk past it wherever you were going.

The ground floor was cosmetics. Attractive men and women with no visible pores or blemishes used this space to casually assault shoppers with expensive bottles of perfumes and face creams. Whatever you came in for, you'd leave the shop smelling like a perfumer after a bad day in the lab.

If you managed to make it through unscathed, a set of escalators whisked you to the first floor, where you'd be greeted by an array of women's clothing. Mostly aimed at a woman of a certain vintage, though more boutiques were opening up that appealed to the younger generations. Their designs were daring and provocative and drew frowns and tuts from the purple-rinsed ladies who'd stopped in for a new plastic rain bonnet.

The second floor was chaos. Appealing odours drifted out from the café into the nursery section. Screams of pleasure (and displeasure) sounded from the ToyTown section, as children's wishes for a new action figure or remote-controlled car were granted or dashed. In the far corner, a harried looking woman was overseeing a calendar stall that looked both temporary and low on stock.

Every surface was covered in twinkling lights and a huge Christmas tree filled the centre of the floor. It looked overblown, and very much like the one in that episode of Mr. Bean where he visits Harrods.

'Do you see him?' Adam asked.

Colin scanned the second floor, but there was still no sign of Kyle.

'The office is in the back,' Colin suggested. 'But I suppose we can't really just walk in there.'

'We could try.'

They spent a few minutes looking around the top floor, and when there was still no trace of the store's owner, they set off towards a set of double doors with STAFF ONLY signs screwed into them.

The doors opened into a small waiting room, manned by a blonde woman sitting behind a desk. She assessed them with catlike eyes, though greeted them with a warm smile.

'Can I help you?' she asked.

Adam looked at Colin, who shrugged and looked right back.

'We're, uh...' Adam started.

'Oh, sorry. Silly me. You're obviously here for the emergency seasonal staff interviews, right?'

'Right,' Adam said, before his brain had time to truly compute what she'd said.

'Mr. Baldwin shouldn't be too much longer. Please, take a seat,' she said, waving a hand at the line of chairs that were sat along a faded cream wall.

'In fact, do you mind if I just nip to the toilet? I'm a bit nervous.' Adam rubbed his stomach and made a face.

'No problem.'

They walked back out of the door and Adam made for the stairs. Colin grabbed the back of his jacket.

'Where are you going?'

'Home?' Adam said.

'What about the interview?'

'What *about* the interview?' Adam repeated. 'Do *you* want a job here?'

'No, but I think you should.'

'What?'

'Think about it. Your gardening work is seasonal, so you have a load of time on your hands. This is a great way to get a bit of extra money, which you'll need for the wedding, and also a good way to keep an eye on Baldwin.'

'We don't even know he's involved.'

'But what if he is?' Colin said. 'This is the perfect way to keep tabs on him.'

Adam knew it was a good opportunity, but explaining it to Helena would be weird. It was the kind of thing they'd discuss first, but he supposed she had a lot of A&E shifts coming up, and he had some spare time. Colin's point about a bit of extra cash in the pocket was a good one, too.

'I haven't prepared anything for an interview, though,' Adam said.

'Just tell him you're willing to work whenever, in whatever department you're needed in. You'll work yourself to the bone for the duration of the Christmas period, and be fully committed to the role for as long as you are employed.'

'Are you sure you don't want the job? Adam laughed.

'Knock 'em dead, tiger.'

'That might be the weirdest thing you've ever said to me,' Adam said, before heading back towards the staff only door.

THE WOMAN BEHIND the desk nodded towards Adam's stomach as he reappeared.

'All okay down there?' she asked.

'All good, thanks.' He felt his face redden somewhat, as he took a seat and waited.

He lifted a battered copy of The Stonebridge Gazette that was lying on one of the other chairs and flicked through it, finding nothing noteworthy. He threw it down again and smiled when he saw the woman looking at him.

'Lauren, by the way,' she said. 'I'm Mr. Baldwin's PA.'

'Adam.'

'Has it been your dream to work in a department store at Christmas?' she laughed.

'For just about as long as I can remember, yeah,' Adam said.

'Tell him that and the job's yours,' she said, winking, before turning back to her laptop.

Lauren was an attractive girl. Adam put her around the thirty-year-old mark. Her long, blonde hair looked silky in the bright, overhead lights and her smile was perfect. Adam wondered if Colin had clocked her, and thought that if he did get the job, maybe he'd try and play matchmaker.

Helena had often commented that it would be nice to have more couples to hang out with.

Baldwin's office door creaked open and a confident looking interviewee walked out. He gave Adam a lingering glare, like a sporting star might give the opposition before a big game. Maybe this dude was trying to psyche Adam out.

Adam chuckled when the guy had gone. If he cared that much about the job, he was welcome to it.

Kyle Baldwin appeared in the doorway. Thick hair slicked back with too much gel, striped shirt straining against the paunch of his belly, the elbows of his designer suit rubbed shiny from overwearing. His tie had little Christmas trees with googly eyes on them, that looked like his wife (if he had one) had convinced him to put it on and he'd succumbed to save an argument.

He looked at Adam, then to Lauren, and back to Adam.

'Can I help you?' he said.

'He's here for the interview,' Lauren said.

'I thought we were done?'

'Apparently not,' she said, motioning to Adam as if unveiling a new car.

'In that case,' Kyle said, motioning to Adam, 'follow me.'

Adam pushed himself up from the chair and did as he was told.

Kyle's office reeked of self-congratulation. Framed photographs of the man himself filled most of the walls; a comprehensive history of his time in charge of the store. These were interspersed with newspaper clippings and magazine articles about his pride and joy. A large window overlooked the main street, and a heavy oak desk filled most of the space, looking out of place in the pokey room.

'Sit, please,' he said, as he squeezed past the desk and sank into his expensive leather chair. 'Can I get you a glass of water?'

'No, I'm okay, thank you,' Adam said.

'In that case, let's begin.'

The interview lasted longer than Adam had been expecting. It started with the basics. Adam apologised for forgetting to bring a CV with him, but talked through his employment to date. He could see Kyle was impressed when he mentioned starting his own business.

After that, it moved on to hypothetical workplace scenarios and what you'd do if they happened. You'd have to be a moron to say the wrong thing, and Adam told him what he wanted to hear.

He watched Kyle tick the sheet of paper on his desk as he spoke, and when he finished, the boss asked the question he'd obviously been dying to ask from the start.

'Why do you want to work at Baldwin's?'

Because I want to know more about why you hired a homeless man as your Santa and not Tom, as per the norm. I also want to spy on you, to see if you had anything to do with Gerald's untimely demise.

That was the real answer. Instead, Adam once again told him what he wanted to hear: That Baldwin's was a Stonebridge institution, and that to work in this great building would be a privilege, nay, an honour. It would allow him to become part of the fabric of a town he loved, even if the job was only for a few weeks.

Something like that, anyway. He might've gone a bit overboard, but it did the trick. Kyle nodded expansively and wiped something from his eye. The man had an ego. When Adam had finished waxing lyrical about the Baldwin empire, Kyle threw this hand out and offered him the job on the spot.

Adam thought of Mr. Psyche-Out and smiled as he shook Kyle's sweaty hand.

8

THE DRUGS DON'T WORK

COLIN'S REGULAR GAME of five-a-side was facing the usual festive disruption. They were increasingly relying on friends of friends to fill the spots at the last minute as Christmas drew nearer, which had its advantages and disadvantages.

It was a good way to meet new people, and most of the lads who played were sociable and good-natured. They saw the game for what it was: a bunch of old friends having a fun time. Sure, occasionally, the odd mistimed tackle caused a few cross words and a bit of handbags, but overall, it was a friendly game.

On the very odd occasion, someone turned up in studded boots (a no-no on the AstroTurf pitch), thinking that they were Stonebridge's answer to Messi. They always ended up souring the game and were never invited back. If you were the one who invited them, you were in the bad books too.

Nick was in the bad books tonight.

His mate Phil—Alice-band holding back longish hair and shin guards so small they may as well have been playing cards— was ruining the game by tackling late, rarely passing the ball, and mouthing off when things didn't go his way.

Colin was furious, and was trying his best not to let it show. He'd been caught by one of Phil's studs on the shin, and blood had been dribbling down his leg since. He wasn't one to let his emotions get the better of him, but he was biding his time until the chance for revenge reared its head.

With ten minutes left, Ross played a ball down the side of the pitch, and Colin saw his chance. As Phil collected the ball, he looked up to assess his options and was subsequently flattened against the wall. It was more of an ice-hockey style tackle, and would've been a straight red in the Premier League.

Here, it received little complaint, and as Phil lay prone, trying to persuade air to enter his lungs, Colin received a few pats on the back as he walked away from the scene of the crime, ready to form a wall for the deserved free kick.

Phil got up a minute later, though his swagger was gone and he steered well clear of Colin for the rest of the game.

At the end, everyone made their way from the pitch to the bar for the customary post-match pint.

By now, with the edge of his competitiveness blunted and justice served, Colin felt bad. He approached Phil, who was sitting in a booth with Nick watching the Champion's League game on the big screen TV, and offered his apologies.

Phil waved them away graciously, though did take Colin up on the offer of a drink, which Colin ordered and brought back to the table.

'Cheers,' he said, clinking glasses.

Talk turned to the game on TV, and to the weekend fixtures, and to how much Phil had won on a bet the previous evening.

At this point, Phil took a packet out of his pocket and laid it on the table. He took some items from it, and Colin saw that he was setting about rolling a joint. The stench of the marijuana hit the back of Colin's nose, and he looked around the room to see if this blatant illegal activity was being clocked by anyone else.

Apparently, he was the only stick-in-the-mud, as everyone else had barely glanced before going on with their conversations. Colin couldn't believe that Phil was being so nonchalant about it.

'Aren't you worried someone will say something?' Colin said.

'Nah,' Phil replied. 'Everyone's at it, aren't they?'

He picked up a filter and placed it in the roll, before sprinkling the little buds in. Once he was finished, he cleared up the table and picked the joint up, placing it behind his ear for later.

'Do you buy from Stu?' Colin asked.

'Usually, aye. Funny story, actually. There was word around campus about a month ago that there was a new dealer on the block. Much cheaper. So, we went and found him, bought from him and went back to halls. The new stuff wasn't doing anything for us, and after a few joints we realised that the new guy had sold us tea. Can you believe that?' he laughed.

'That is ballsy. Did he not think you'd notice?'

'I don't know what he was thinking.' Phil took a sizeable gulp of his pint. 'But we thought we'd go and teach him a lesson. We were a hundred quid down.'

'I thought you said he was cheaper?'

'Twenty for a big bag is decent. Stu would be charging closer to forty. Should've known it was too good to be true. Anyway, me and my friends had been drinking, but we go looking for this geezer, plan to show him what's what.'

He took another hit of his pint, and Colin had the distinct impression that Phil had watched one too many Guy Ritchie films in his lifetime. He'd never heard someone from Stonebridge use the word geezer, but then he didn't run in circles that bought drugs and doled out punishments, either.

'And did you show him what's what?'

'We did. Gave him a bit of a duffing. Nothing too much, you know. When he was on the ground, we found his money and took back what he'd taken from us. And a wee bit more for the trouble he'd caused us.'

'Did you kill him?' Colin whispered.

'Oh, God no,' Phil said, looking sideways at him. 'Jesus, it was only twenty quid each. I'm not bloody Scarface.'

'You're sure he was alive when you left him?'

'Sure. He was pushing himself back up when we were leaving, turning the air blue with the names he was calling us.'

Colin didn't need to ask who the new dealer was. He assumed the stricken man was Gerald, and wouldn't put it past the fella to put tea in a bag and pass it off as weed. Not many people would go and challenge him when they figured they'd been tricked.

But, Phil's retribution had been a month ago. Gerald only died last week, so Colin figured that the pocket-Ronaldo next to him had nothing to do with his actual death.

It certainly begged a question, though.

Who else had Gerald Agnew wronged?

9

FIRST DAY JITTERS

ADAM POURED A bowl of cereal for himself, and one for Helena. He carried it from their kitchen to the living room, where his wife-to-be (if she said yes when he finally got around to asking the question) was sitting on the sofa.

He handed her the bowl and she pressed play on the next episode of Superstore. For the next twenty minutes, they watched and ate, before Adam got up.

'I still can't believe you got a job without telling me,' she laughed.

'It was all a bit quick,' he replied.

'You're telling me!'

'I just thought that the extra money wouldn't go amiss, you know? Plus, you're working all hours. At least this way I can't get myself into mischief.'

'More mischief, you mean. How is the case going?'

'Not sure, really. There are a couple of suspects who could've been behind it, but it's hard to narrow it down.'

'Stu?'

Adam had been filling Helena in on the breaking news as they got it.

'He's one of them,' Adam nodded. 'Didn't like that there was another dealer on his patch. Colin just told me about some lad he played football with last night who beat Gerald up a month or so ago, but I don't think he's in the frame. Then there is Tom Little, the regular Santa, and Kyle Baldwin.'

'Why would Kyle kill the man he'd only recently hired as his new Santa, though?'

'See?' Adam said, throwing his hands in the air. 'None of it makes sense. If it wasn't for the footprints in the picture you took, I'd be agreeing with the police that it was just a nasty accident.'

'But you don't think it is, right? So, what's next?'

'Not sure. I'm going to ask around at work, see if Kyle and Gerald had any beef. Maybe Kyle regretted what he'd done in not hiring Tom, went to tell Gerald he'd made a mistake, and the two got into an argument.'

'Sounds unlikely,' Helena said.

And she was right. None of it was seeming likely right now. They needed to either start asking the right questions, or accept that DI Whitelaw knew what he was doing. There was a first time for everything, after all.

He kissed her on the forehead and went to the bedroom to get dressed for his first day.

BY LUNCHTIME, he was regretting ever having walked into that backroom and accepting the job.

The crowds were mental.

His hands were hurting from folding so many clothes and he didn't know where anything was yet, so received many snooty remarks from little old ladies in a hurry, like he was some sort of usurper in their cherished store.

Whoever was in charge of the sound system had played the same five Christmas songs on loop. In his three hours of works, he'd heard *It's Beginning To Look A Lot Like Christmas* twelve times.

Twelve!

He was beginning to think that anyone who worked here could be behind Gerald Agnew's killing. Surely hearing that song that many times in one shift was enough to drive anyone to murder.

He was thankful when his break time came around. He escaped off the floor and into the staffroom, where three others were engaged in a heated debate. He shuffled past them and pulled his sandwiches from the fridge, and when he looked up all eyes were on him. An old lady with white hair, who introduced herself as Carol, had just finished talking and they looked like they expected him to join in.

'What are you talking about?' Adam asked, sitting down near them.

'We're discussing the weirdest body part,' Carol said. 'Nancy thinks it's body hair and I think it's the bones in your ear.'

'Which is ridiculous,' argued a young man with the beginnings of a moustache. 'They do a vital job. Whereas, the milk teeth are the stupidest thing known to man.'

'Explain.'

'Well, they hurt babies like a bitch and only last six years or something. And when they fall out it's equally as distressing.'

'So, what would you suggest as an alternative?' Carol asked.

'Metal teeth that last a lifetime,' concluded the moustachioed man.

Adam reckoned he had given this argument a lot of thought, and had practiced the finer points over a milkshake or two with his friends. If he had any, which Adam thought unlikely.

'So?' they said, rounding on him.

'I'm not sure, really. I'll give it some thought and get back to you.'

Silence descended upon the room, so Adam ate his food. When he had finished, he asked the others: 'What do you reckon to this business with Gerald Agnew?'

'Who?' the boy said.

Carol seemed to be in charge of this rag-tag group, as she spoke for them. She shushed the boy with a withering look.

'The people who work here were very confused as to what Kyle was thinking, though of course we'd never say that to him. We'd be out on our ears. We also felt very sorry for poor Tom, who would've been celebrating a landmark occasion had he been chosen. There was talk of walkouts, in solidarity, but…'

'You'd rather keep your job than show your support,' Adam said.

'Well, when you put it like that.'

'What's Kyle like?' Adam asked.

'He's a lovely man. Cares about the company.' She cast an eye around as if he might be listening through the walls, before whispering, 'But he will occasionally do things that raise an eyebrow.'

'And they always seem to come after he's had a meeting with his father, who is still on the board of directors,' added Nancy.

'What kinds of things?' Adam asked.

'Moving the boutiques around, which confuses the old dears. Changing the menu in the café, which also confuses the old dears,' Carol smiled. 'Generally upsetting the old dears, I suppose you could say.'

'No one here wanted Gerald to be the Santa,' Nancy chimed in, seemingly annoyed that Carol was pussyfooting around the issue. 'Tom was made for the role—natural beard, white hair, a bit round. Whereas, Gerald is a big stringy fella who reeks of BO. Hardly the message you want to send out to the children who come to visit.'

'But no one challenged him?' Adam asked, causing the three to look sheepish. He got up to leave. 'Oh, one last question. Who do I talk to about the playlist?'

LAUREN WAS WHERE she was last time Adam had seen her— behind the little desk outside Kyle's office. She wiped at her eyes as he pushed his way through the door, and greeted him with a smile that looked painted on.

'You okay?' he asked. 'Sorry, I didn't mean to barge in.'

'Oh, yeah. Sorry, just something silly. Don't worry.'

'You sure? Anything I can help with?'

'No, honestly, I'm grand,' she said. 'What's up with you? Don't tell me you're quitting already.'

'I might be if someone doesn't fix the playlist,' he replied.

'Ah, that. We have this argument every year. Kyle likes to keep the playlist short and sweet and on repeat. Thinks our demographic find the repetitive nature of the songs comforting.'

'Whereas the people who work here find it drives one of the unpacking knives closer to their wrists each time Justin Bieber's *Mistletoe* starts again.'

She laughed at that.

'Look, I'll see what I can do. I might be able to sneak one extra song a day in there. Gotta take it slow or he'll be onto us, although he's been a bit distracted the past week or so, so we might get away with it.'

'We?' Adam repeated.

'Well, yeah. I mean, *I'm* perfectly happy with the playlist.' She winked. 'But I'll change it for you, if it makes you happy.'

'It would,' he nodded. 'Start with The Darkness.'

'Oh, let's not go crazy. Some of our clientele might drop dead at the sound of wailing guitars. We'll compromise on *Wonderful Christmastime.*'

They laughed again, causing Kyle to open his door and check on the cause of the merriment. His suit was an outlandish red tartan today.

'What's going on?' he asked.

'Oh, Adam's just telling me about some of the shenanigans on the shop floor today.'

'You're enjoying it, then?' Kyle asked, suddenly beaming, and Adam nodded.

'Oh, before I go,' Adam said, turning back to Lauren. 'I meant to ask, if it's not too weird, if you're single? My friend, who I was in with yesterday, was very complimentary, is all.'

'That's very sweet,' she smiled.

Adam glanced across at Kyle, who was looking at her like he wanted to know the answer to the question, too, which struck him as a little creepy. The man was probably fifteen years her senior, and a little more on top. She glanced across at him before answering, like she'd been aware of his gaze.

'As it goes, I am,' she said.

10

THE SCENE OF THE CRIME
(IF IT WAS A CRIME TO BEGIN WITH)

UNSURE OF WHAT to do next, Adam and Colin did what they normally do—filled their bellies and hoped the sheer amount of greasy breakfast food would lend them some inspiration.

It didn't.

All it did was make them sluggish.

Colin sat back in his chair and wished he could undo a button on his trousers.

'Do you think we just sack it all off?' Adam asked. 'It feels like it's going nowhere.'

'It does feel like that,' he agreed. 'But we've never given up on any of the others. Why this one?'

'With the others, it was clear that there was definitely a crime. With this… I don't know. Maybe he did just slip.'

'Maybe. But what about the footprints? They must count for something.'

'The footprints are the only thing stopping me from throwing the towel in, however much I want to.' Adam went to scoop a mouthful of beans into his mouth, but stopped halfway, setting the fork down again.

'We've been through the suspects again, but no one stands out. Maybe we go and have a look at the spot where you found him?'

'Could do. Won't the police have been through his stuff?'

'Not if they are as dim-witted as they usually are. If they were convinced what happened to him was an accident, I reckon they'll have left his bedding and stuff like that.'

'Worth a look,' Adam said.

They got up and paid at the till, before waddling out of the shop and heading towards the alley. On the way, Adam told Colin about Lauren's availability and, at first, Colin berated him for mentioning his name. However, the more Colin ruminated on that little nugget, the more he started to smile.

Kyle's PA was beautiful, and Adam said she seemed a bit of a laugh, too.

He apologised to Adam for going off on one, and asked for more details, of which there weren't many.

'Except,' Adam said, 'I got her number for you.'

He pulled out his phone and read the number aloud, while Colin typed the digits into his phonebook and saved it. He'd text her later, once he'd had time to think about what he was going to say.

The simple "hey" of yesteryear was seen as lazy. You needed a USP, at least in the world of online dating.

'What should I say?' he asked.

'Just ask her out for a drink or something,' Adam replied. 'Keep it simple.'

If he'd known ten years ago that Adam Whyte would be giving him dating advice, Colin might have ended it all there and then.

Still, he was thankful that his friend was being a good wingman. He thanked him again as they turned into the alley where Adam had almost stumbled over the body of Gerald Agnew.

THE ALLEY LOOKED different in the cold light of day.

Of course, that was, in large part, down to the fact that there was no body now. But there were other differences, too. The snow had melted, exposing the ground and the graffiti looked less urban and cool than it did at night; now it looked like the deranged scrawling of a talentless lunatic.

Adam and Colin walked up the narrow alley and stood by the pole. The blood had been washed off, but that wasn't what Adam was looking at—he was studying the ground.

Small metal studs surrounded the pole, driven into the ground. Adam had seen these before in areas where slippage might occur, and knew they were there to create friction with your shoe.

The snow that night had just fallen. It was fluffy and soft, so was in no way a slipping hazard. Adam pointed out the little metallic domes and explained his thinking. Colin nodded along.

'Let's have a look at where he was sleeping.'

They walked a few more steps down the alley and looked into the little nook where Gerald had been calling home.

There was a nervous looking old man in there, his earthly belongings scattered around a frayed and filthy sleeping bag. He appraised them with bloodshot, worried eyes and began to stammer.

'Don't make me move, officers. It's cosy and…'

Adam cut him off.

'We're not police. You're safe. We're just looking for Gerald's stuff.'

'Why?'

'We're looking into his death.'

'That's good of you boys,' he said. 'Gerald was a pal, and I know he'd be happy with me taking his place.'

'Isn't it Marty's place?'

'In a matter of speaking, but he won big at the poker and is treating himself to a couple of nights in a guest house. Said I could have his spot in exchange for a few ciggies. Nice for some, isn't it?'

'Has anyone been to look through Gerald's things? Police?'

'Nah, no one. And I'm an honest gentleman, you understand? I've not touched anything, except the fags, 'cos he's not going to need them where he's gone. Everything else is there as he left it.'

'What's your name?'

The man swept a hand through his thick mane and seemed to consider whether the question was a trick one. Seemingly, he didn't think so, though he still appeared cagey when he told them he was called Mick.

'Nice to meet you, Mick,' Adam said, as he began poking through the remnants of Gerald's life, which didn't amount to much.

There was a busking hat and a guitar with all but one of the strings missing. An old, tattered sleeping bag and an ancient MP3 player that had been drained of battery many moons ago. A heavy winter coat that the paramedics must've thought another homeless person could make use of, so tossed it back on his pile before they'd carted him off.

Adam peeled back the sleeping bag, and found a number of small bags of weed. Or what looked like weed, at least. It could well have been tea, going on Gerald's past form.

'Were there any more of these?' he asked.

'What are you trying to say?' Mick said, looking affronted.

'I'm not accusing you of anything, man. I'm only asking if these were all the drugs Gerald had.'

'As far as I know. I've been here constantly, pretty much since he died, and no one has touched anything, and I've certainly not. Marty wasn't even interested. He's into the harder stuff.'

'Haven't you considered selling it?'

'And have Stu Finnegan all over me? No thank you, sir. I'd rather keep my face the way it is.'

'Did he have words with Gerald, do you know?'

'Aye, he had words alright, but that was that, in fairness. Or so I was told. When we saw him coming down the road, we all scarpered. Gerald stood firm, and I think Stu could see that he wasn't going to need a duffing. That he was a reasonable man. That this was his turf.'

'And that was that?'

'Aye.'

'Do you know who Gerald was selling to?'

'He wasn't at it for very long. His heart wasn't in it, to be fair. Who is going to buy drugs off a tramp? He did sell some to a couple of the wee uni lads and did the dirty on them. Paid the price for that with a black eye and a couple of sore ribs.'

'And they left him after that?'

'Aye. That old man who used to be Santa came down a couple of times, but Gerald refused to sell to him. Thought 'cos he had taken his Baldwin's gig that the old Santa was trying to buy drugs and then get him in trouble, so he told the guy where to go.'

Adam thought about that for a while. They'd spoken to Tom and he'd never mentioned anything about visiting Gerald with the intention of buying drugs. Maybe they should speak to him again.

They thanked Mick for his help, and turned to leave.

'It's a shame poor Gerald has passed on. He seemed excited about the future, you know? Said he had irons in the fire and that, with any luck, he'd be off the streets by new year.'

'What did he mean?' Adam asked.

'Beats me,' Mick replied, cracking open a bottle of cheap cider.

They figured the fizz of the Frosty Jack's signalled the end of Mick's helpfulness, and left him to it.

11

ANOTHER LITTLE MEETING

TOM PUSHED HIS plate away and wiped his lips with a napkin, making sure to be thorough. Tomato soup was a no-go during his Santa days, for fear of spilling some onto his white beard. It wouldn't do well to greet a child warmly, only to be met with a horrified expression when their small little mind mistook soup for blood. Zombie Santa was not a good look.

Now that he wasn't bound with the chains of St. Nick, and with the cold weather zeroing in on his old bones, he could do whatever he liked, and that included having two bowls of forbidden soup at lunch if he wanted.

He smiled to himself and pulled the paper closer, though there wasn't much going on in the town. A few drink driving offenders were being made an example of in the run up to Christmas, which he saw as a good thing. Aside from that, the only thing that interested him was that Stonebridge FC had lost to local rivals (again) in football, and the manager was bullish about the prospects of being fired in his press conference.

The sooner he left, the better, Tom thought.

And then, all thoughts deserted him as two familiar faces walked into his little slice of sanctuary. He lifted the paper high, covering his face, in the hope that he hadn't been spotted.

ADAM AND COLIN closed the door behind them, keeping the cold breeze locked out. They'd watched Tom enter the café about twenty minutes ago and hoped to catch him on the way out, make it seem like it was a chance encounter.

Unfortunately, Adam had to get back to work, and thus Father Time had forced them to act.

They slipped into the chairs opposite and Tom lowered the paper, resignation plastered across his face.

'I assume this isn't a coincidence?' he asked, setting the paper aside.

'Correct,' Colin said. 'We thought another little chat might be useful. You see, we've heard whispers about you.'

Tom looked genuinely confused.

'Not here, lads. Too many ears,' he said. 'Let's go for a walk.'

Tom left them and approached the counter, paying his bill and putting on a jolly show for two small children who were sat near the till. He may not be the official Baldwin's Santa, but he was still the closest thing Stonebridge had. As he walked away, the children were positively vibrating in their seats and their mother had a huge grin plastered across her face.

'Shall we?' he asked, when he'd wrapped himself up.

They left the café, and the shrill bite of the wind was most unwelcome as they stepped out onto the bustling street.

'Last time you told us you had no beef with Gerald,' Colin said. 'That you hadn't been to see him.'

'Beef?'

'You know, no problems, no ill-feeling.'

'Ah. Why beef?'

'I don't know,' Adam shrugged.

'So, why were you visiting him?' Colin said, hoping not to get bogged down in the origin of slang.

'I wasn't. I hadn't,' Tom spluttered.

'It might look, to the police, let's say,' Colin shrugged, 'that you claiming you hadn't been anywhere near him and evidence emerging that you in fact *had* been to see him, as troublesome.'

'Evidence?'

'Eye-witness. Saw you a couple of times.'

'Okay, okay. I went to see him a few weeks after he'd been announced, but it wasn't on Santa business. It was to do with…' He looked around to make sure no one was nearby and listening in. '…Drugs.'

'Drugs?'

'I've got terrible glaucoma. I've been on all sorts of medication, and none of it is helping. I can feel my eyesight going, and it's a scary feeling—I wouldn't wish it on my worst enemy. One of the young boys in work was telling me that, in America, medical marijuana is prescribed for it. So, I thought I'd go and see him.'

'But he thought you were trying to frame him. Buy the drugs and then go grass him up.'

'And why would I do that?'

'Don't be naïve,' Colin laughed. 'You dob him in, he loses the job and the money, and you get your throne back.'

'Money?'

'Yeah, the money for being Santa.'

Tom laughed. 'Boys, I've been the big man for many years and I've not received a penny for my troubles. It's more of a pride thing.'

'But Gerald was getting paid for it. That's what we were told.'

'And look where it got him,' Tom sighed. 'And now, if there really is nothing else, I hope I don't see you two again in the near future.'

They watched him walk away towards his place of temporary work, and Adam pulled his coat sleeve up to check the time.

'Balls,' he said. 'I'm going to be late if I don't get a wiggle on.'

'No worries,' Colin said. 'I'll see you soon.'

Colin headed back towards the café they'd been in with Tom, his stomach rumbling at the thought of a big lunch. He sat down at the same table, which had now been cleared, and perused the menu.

When the waitress came, he ordered a Christmas dinner with all the trimmings, and then pulled his phone out.

He went to the messages and composed a new missive to Lauren. It took him a while to word it correctly, not wanting to come across as too keen or too aloof, and when he was happy, he re-read it a couple more times to make sure it was actually okay.

Before he could chicken out, he pressed send and then put his phone back in his pocket. He couldn't stand glancing at it every couple of seconds to see if the message had been read, or if there was a reply.

Instead, he picked up the paper and skimmed it. The smell of food wafting from the open kitchen was mouth-watering, and he wished it would hurry up, though upon flicking through a few more pages, the smell of meat and potatoes cooking was suddenly the last thing on his mind.

Buried deep within the paper was a mention of Stu Finnegan. There was no photo, but there were some details. Apparently, he had been caught beating up a student at Stonebridge University's campus. Stu claimed the guy owed him money, which turned out to be less than £20. The guy who owed the money was in hospital with a fractured eye-socket, though was also in trouble for buying drugs in the first place.

Talk about adding insult to injury.

Colin took a photo of the story and closed the paper.

Stu Finnegan had told Adam that he never needed to resort to violence, or something to that effect. He had definitely said he was in no way involved with what had happened to Gerald. Mick had backed that up, but had also been slurping from a giant bottle of cheap cider, so could they take his words as gospel?

Surely if Stu was willing to batter someone for the sake of seventeen pounds, he'd be more than ready to engage in physical violence with someone who was undercutting him and muscling in on his empire.

Colin didn't fancy broaching the subject with the maniac drug dealer, and hoped that the police might get a confession out of him while they were holding him in the cells.

His phone buzzed and what appeared on screen knocked all thoughts of Gerald, Stu and fractured bones out of his head.

He had a message from Lauren and it ended with two kisses.

12

THE PROPOSAL (PART DEUX)

THE GROUNDS OF The Rose Gardens were vast and beautiful. In the centre of the estate sat a large manor house, its balustrades, towers and turrets harking back to a grander time. Intricately carved grotesques guarded each corner of the old stone building. Inside was accessible by the wide, wooden door, currently being guarded by a National Trust volunteer who was shivering despite her thick woollen coat.

The endless blue sky and the light dusting of snow that coated the herbaceous borders and manicured lawns lent the scene a postcard quality, which pleased Adam enormously. It was the perfect scene to describe when answering the 'How did he propose?' question.

Adam and his unsuspecting wife-to-be took an easy stroll through the famous rose gardens. Of course, because it was winter, the vibrancy and definition of the flowers were not at peak beauty, but there was still something wonderful about the colours and the shapes.

There were other people milling about, scarves knotted around necks and coffees in hand, though Adam was trying his best to zone everyone else out.

While Helena was reading an information board about the formation of the gardens and how the owner nearly went bankrupt while trying to fulfil his dream, Adam patted his pocket and pulled the ring box out. With tears in his eyes, he lowered himself down on the grass behind her, the life-changing words on his lips. Something soft and wet squelched under his knee.

The stench of dog dirt reached his nose and made him retch. Thankfully, he had the presence of mind to stow the ring in his pocket before he choked audibly.

Helena turned around to find Adam on the ground, checking the soggy mess on his best trousers.

'What's up?' she asked, nose wrinkled.

'I was tying my bloody shoelace and I landed in this pile of…' Adam motioned to the immense stain. 'What a nightmare.'

'It's okay, we can go to the café and get you cleaned up. You can splash some soap onto it.'

More like set fire to them, he thought, though didn't argue. He needed to propose today, and if it meant doing it with slightly dirty trousers, that would have to do. Maybe it would be funny in those future retellings, though he didn't think so.

They walked back towards the more modern building which housed the café, and went in. The exposed metal work and glass walls allowed uninterrupted views of the landscape. Helena ordered a hot chocolate and settled in the corner, while Adam excused himself.

In the toilets, he pumped what felt like gallons of soap onto the desecrated area and wiped at it with a thick wad of cloth. Instead of coming off, the soap simply made the mess runnier and—if possible—smellier. Now it smelt like poo with top notes of harsh chemical.

Cursing, he held his knee to the air dryer for a while, spreading the stench of the muck around the confined space. He apologised to the other guy at the sink, who wrinkled his nose and left.

Helena grimaced as he sat down, and offered him a sip of her drink. He suggested they continue their walk, and she nodded. They walked outside, the stink following them, and bumped into Colin, who wasn't alone.

'What have we here, then?' Adam asked, introducing Helena to Lauren.

'He was very persistent,' Lauren said, rolling her eyes comically. Colin gave her a playful shove. It seemed they'd already become comfortable with one another.

'Thought we'd come for a wee walk,' Colin said. 'What happened to your knee?'

'He fell foul of dog excrement,' Helena answered.

'Nasty.' Colin pulled a face. 'You going home now?'

'We we're going to go for a walk too.' Helena said.

'We could make up a foursome?' Colin suggested.

Adam moved slightly behind Helena and shook his head, holding up his ring finger. Before Colin could reply, Lauren spoke.

'Aren't you supposed to be in work today, Adam?'

'I don't think so,' Adam said.

'The rota got changed. Didn't you get the email? Shirley was sick and Freddie jacked it in, so you were needed today, I think.' She pulled out her phone and scrolled through some emails, before holding it up to him. 'You're supposed to start at 1.'

'Balls,' he said, checking his watch. He only had an hour to get home, get changed and get to Baldwin's. Lauren apologised for being the bearer of bad news.

'Sorry,' he said to Helena, before bidding goodbye to Lauren and Colin and hightailing it back to the car.

HEAVY TRAFFIC AND slow walkers combined to make Adam late for work. He'd checked his watch nervously as he'd tried to shuffle his way past the walking dead of Stonebridge, and had decided that if he was going to be late, which he was, he'd simply slope onto the shop floor and pretend that he wasn't late at all—that'd he'd been here for a while and had forgotten to sign in.

Sadly, that plan was highjacked by Kyle, who was standing by the escalator looking at his own, much more expensive watch. Adam tried to glide past him on the moving stairs, but Kyle beckoned him back, causing Adam to have to walk backwards one step each time the stairs moved to keep stationary.

'What time do you call this?' he asked, as Adam lapsed into a sort of mechanical moonwalk.

'1:03pm.'

'And what time am I paying you from?'

'1pm.'

'Hmmm, that leaves me in a quandary,' Kyle said, adopting a pensive look. 'What to do? What to do?'

'Don't pay me for those three minutes,' Adam suggested.

'No, no. I'm an honest man and I'd rather give you the money than not.'

'There's no problem, then, is there?' Adam said, his mood darkening. He stopped treading the steps and let them sweep him up to the next floor. He stored his stuff in his locker and made his way to ladieswear, where he began mindlessly folding and hanging the clothes that had been abandoned after being tried on in the changing rooms.

He didn't have to be here. The job was a cover to get information about Kyle's involvement with Gerald Agnew, and he could jack it in right now. Tell the boss where to stick his job and his precious three minutes.

But, upon reflection, he felt like he hadn't made the most of the opportunities he'd been handed to their full potential. He had a wealth of workers here who knew Kyle better than most, and he'd barely spoken to any of them. Most employees had some sort of gripe against their boss, and it was time to exploit that.

For the rest of his shift, he broke the mould. He walked around, doing what he needed to do, but had a couple of insightful chats at the same time.

Tina in cookery implied Kyle had a temper.

Alison in home electronics conceded that, once, she'd heard Kyle scream at an employee in his office because his coffee was delivered cold.

Konrad in gardening cast a few furtive glances around, before telling Adam that Kyle was a straight-up... four letter word. Adam blushed as he thanked him for his insight.

It was helpful stuff, but then something occurred to him. Lauren would surely be a fount of knowledge—everyone bitched about their boss. He made a beeline for the back room, but Lauren's desk was empty. He made a mental note to catch her at some stage, and headed back to the shop floor.

And, as time ticked toward his shift ending, Adam felt a bit better. He had a background now, and he fully believed that Kyle had something to do with Gerald's death. It was too suspicious that the year he got picked to be Santa for the store, something bad happened to him. Especially when taking his chequered history into consideration.

Now, he just needed hard evidence.

On his way out, Kyle stopped him and apologised for being pedantic that afternoon. Stress, he said. This time of year always got to him. Adam held up a placating hand and told him he knew how it was, and not to worry, and that *he* was sorry for his tardiness. He started towards the door, before turning back.

'I'm assuming the Santa position is up for grabs now?'

'You're a bit young, son,' Kyle laughed, and Adam joined in, though it was a feeble attempt at humour.

'My granda said he might be interested, depending on the moolah.'

'Ah, sadly, we don't pay. Tom did it for two decades and was glad to do it for the pride of saying he was the Baldwin Santa.'

'Grand. It's just, I heard Gerald was getting some money for it.'

'Who told you that?' Kyle asked, tersely.

'Can't remember.'

'Look,' he said, softening. 'We didn't want it getting out, but we were paying Gerald to see if we could get him off the street. You know what they say about charity?'

'It begins at home?'

'Well, that, too. But I meant, if you broadcast it, it ain't charity. That's why we kept it quiet.'

He slapped Adam's face, twice. The first was light and playful and the second had a bit of venom behind it, or so it seemed. Perhaps Adam imagined it, but his cheek certainly stung as he made his way out into the darkening street.

'See you tomorrow,' Adam said.

13

FINNEGAN'S PLACE

COLIN'S FIRST DATE with Lauren went well. At least, *he* thought it did.

They'd stomped through acres of woodland before enjoying a slice of cake and a mug of tea in the café. Lauren was a good laugh and easy to talk to; didn't mind taking the mick out of herself, which Colin enjoyed. She was also beautiful, and after a few hours together, he could feel the excitement bubbling in his stomach, though he was trying to contain himself, in case she didn't feel the same way.

He'd suggested meeting up again as they'd got into their cars and she'd seemed keen. He'd suggested a few dates, and she'd said that she'd need to check her calendar as she knew she had a few nights out planned with old friends and things like that. Christmas is a busy time, you know how it is, she'd said. It wasn't a no, but a second date hadn't yet been confirmed.

Now, he sat at home, heating on full blast in an effort to get some warmth into his body. The television was on, but he wasn't really watching. He was thinking about his day. Little snapshots kept creeping into his mind, and his face hurt from smiling.

He flicked through the photos they'd taken, and found himself hoping that his camera roll would have more of them together. He'd even considered phoning his mum to tell her about his day, but reckoned he'd save the news until they'd seen each other a few more times.

He'd not thought about Gerald Agnew all day, though that changed when the photos he'd been scrolling through stopped being of snowy gardens and changed to the newspaper story he'd snapped a picture of—the student with the fractured eye socket and the detained dealer.

Stu Finnegan was never going to admit to laying a finger on the dead man, but perhaps there was some way to get him to talk when he got out of the police station. Maybe he'd see the light and turn his back on his criminal enterprises.

Yeah right, Colin thought.

And then he had another thought.

If Stu was incarcerated until his questioning was done with, maybe there was some sort of evidence in his flat or house or wherever he lived that would link him to the murder.

Maybe he'd made it look like he'd bashed Gerald's head off the pole in the alleyway, when actually he'd socked him over the head with a wrench and then made it look like the tramp had had a little slip and fall.

Breaking into Stu's house was madness, but Colin couldn't help but feel that the dealer was somehow involved. Also, he and Adam had spoken briefly this evening, and had arranged a gentleman's bet. Adam thought Kyle was the guilty party, while Colin was convinced it was Stu. Neither wanted to lose and sometimes, the urge to be the winner overpowers common sense.

Maybe the love of a woman was giving him a sense of confidence he usually didn't have. Whatever the case, he'd made up his mind. And anyway, Stu wasn't going to be there, so there'd be no danger involved.

Before that, though, there was something else he felt he should do.

THE HOSPITAL'S ATTEMPT to inject some Christmas cheer was half-hearted at best. Colin supposed that overworked doctors and nurses had been entrusted with the job, and it was the best they could do with the time they could spare.

He walked to the reception and asked where his friend was being kept. He'd memorised the name from the newspaper story and, when he held up a wrapped present and adopted a glum face, the nurse directed him to Joe's ward.

A waiting list for surgery had kept Joe in for more days than he'd have liked, judging by his expression when Colin walked in. It started with a morose look, that gave way to fear when he took in Colin's height and black clothes.

'Don't hurt me,' he said. 'I've paid. I've paid.'

'I'm not here to hurt you,' Colin soothed. 'I'm here to help.'

Colin introduced himself, before taking the chair beside the bed and setting the present on the side table.

'What's that?' Joe asked.

'It's only a couple of beers. But I reckon you could do with one after what you've been through.'

Colin nodded at his face, which was puffy around the nose and as black as night around the left eye. The lid drooped over the swollen skin, looking positively grotesque.

'Sore?' Colin asked.

'Was at the time, aye. That plank got me right and good.'

Joe spoke with a light Dublin lilt, and even when he was describing the attack to Colin, it sounded dreamlike. No wonder the Irish accent got voted sexiest in the world in so many polls.

'You had no idea he was going to get violent?'

'No idea at all. I'd sent him a few texts saying I was going to be getting money at Christmas from me ma, and that he'd get paid then. He said that was grand, and then he turns up one night and breaks my face.'

'No warning.'

'Nope. Right hook to me nose, couple of kicks to the head and it's goodnight, Irene. Took thirty quid out of my pocket while I was unconscious, too. Luckily, my mate saw what happened and videoed it from behind a wall. He apologised later for not running to my aid, but reckoned that having a film of it would be more helpful.'

'Looks like it has been.'

'Aye, the police have been. Said they got him, but that I'm in trouble too for buying. Me ma's going to be so impressed when she sees me!'

Joe's gloominess had given way to something approaching happiness during the time they spoke. Maybe it was sharing the story with someone who wasn't going to judge, or maybe something else. Colin was just glad that he was able to help in some small way.

Colin got up to leave, and before he did, told Joe what he was planning to do. Joe confirmed what Colin was thinking: that it was madness, but that it *could* yield results. Joe had read about Gerald, but told Colin that Stu had never mentioned his name, though why would he?

'Can I have your number?' Joe asked.

'Why?' Colin said.

'You've been kind to me, and I'd like to know that you're alive when the night's over.'

THE IMPULSE THAT something was to be discovered within the walls of Stu Finnegan's home was waning now that Colin was outside. Wisely, he'd walked—not trusting that he'd park up and actually do this if he'd taken the car.

He imagined Adam, lambasting him for doing something so stupid, but his friend was so convinced of Kyle Baldwin's guilt that Colin feared he'd chucked all his eggs in one basket.

He'd paced the street for the best part of twenty minutes and hadn't met another soul. On the last Friday before Christmas, most were at work parties or down the boozer with old friends they hadn't seen in a while.

And here was Colin, with only the waning moon, the glittering stars, and a grotty street full of terraced houses for company. He considered what he was doing one more time before walking up the steps to Stu's house and knocking.

He'd spoken to Gaz, their police officer friend earlier, who told him Stu was still behind bars. Colin hung up before Gaz could ask any more questions. He wasn't a fan of Adam and Colin's extra-curricular activities and certainly wouldn't approve of Colin's current plan.

Of course, a lot could happen in a few hours where the law is concerned. A minute after Colin had hung up, Stu could've been turned loose. If the front door opened and Stu appeared, Colin would run. That was his thinking.

However, the door did not open, so Colin hurried down an alley filled with bins and into the back garden, where he was met with a locked door and a window that had been left open. The stench of weed drifted out of it, and Colin supposed that Stu had left it open to air the place, intending to return a little while after. Instead, he'd battered someone half to death and the police had picked him up.

The garden had been left to rot and ruin—a gardener's hand had not been felt there since the trees had been planted. The bare branches stretched into the sky like spindly fingers, and did a good job of keeping nosy neighbours from being able to see very much at all. Add in the inky blackness of the night, and Colin may as well have been a ghost.

He cast a glance around, just to make sure there wasn't a hidden CCTV camera or a lurking rottweiler, though if there was, he'd probably have known about it by now. That particular breed of dog isn't renowned for its sneakiness.

Happy that he was alone, he swung a foot onto the windowsill and, using a gloved hand, pulled the window further open. He clambered in and landed with little grace in the living room.

It was a mess. Every surface was littered with empty beer cans and equipment used for weighing, bagging and selling drugs. The sofa was at an odd angle, as if there'd been a recent struggle, and a bright blue light from the television bathed the room in an alien hue.

Colin set to work, not really knowing what he was looking for, besides something incriminating. Of course, the room was full of incriminating things that could land Stu in lots of trouble, but after a fruitless search, Colin concluded that the murder weapon was not among them.

The knives in the kitchen were not soaked in Gerald's blood, and there was no hammer, or wrench, or screwdriver dripping with the dead man's DNA.

Colin ascended the stairs. The small landing was faced with three doors, all shut, which brought an uncomfortable level of darkness. He reached for his phone and accessed the torch function, which lit up the space quite intensely.

Colin nearly fell backwards down the stairs as the torch's beam illuminated a pair of bright green eyes. A steady stream of four lettered words spewed forth from Colin's mouth, even after he'd realised it was only a little tabby cat.

The cat, for his part, was unmoved and unoffended by Colin's profanities, neither their content nor the sheer volume. Colin supposed afterwards that the cat *was* living with a drug-addled maniac and was probably used to far worse.

Bending down, Colin reached out and stroked the cat's head. It accepted the fuss, before slinking past Colin's legs and making its way down the stairs. Colin watched it go and then searched each of the rooms, again to no avail.

It had been a stupid idea to come here. He closed the final bedroom door behind him and froze as he heard a key slide into the lock of the front door.

The lock clicked, the door swung open and slammed again a moment later. Heavy footsteps sounded on the wooden floorboards in the hallway and a voice drifted up the stairs.

Panic seized Colin in a vice-like grip. He looked around wildly, ruling out the bathroom and bedroom as hiding places. Stu was likely to use those in the near future. Instead, Colin quietly opened the door to the airing cupboard and squeezed himself in beside the boiler. He pulled the door closed again and waited.

A few minutes later, the voice grew louder. There were gaps in the conversation and Colin realised that Stu must've been on the phone. He strained his ears, and caught a snatch of the exchange.

'I needed a dump, so I've stopped off at Stu's… Aye, I know, but he's in jail…. Don't worry. He's not going to know that I've dropped a depth charge down his bog. Might not even flush. Merry Christmas, pal.'

Peals of deep, booming laughter filled the landing and Colin readied himself. He heard the bathroom door open and the lock click, and as the first splash sounded, he bounded from his hiding place and nearly took the stairs in one leap. He span left and ran to the front door, which thankfully the mystery man in the toilet had left unlocked.

He sprinted out of the gate, and kept running until his lungs turned against him and there were tears in his eyes. He hadn't dared to look back, but reckoned that whoever was in the bathroom had either stayed there or had been too slow to catch a sighting.

Colin shook his head at his own stupidity and walked home on mutinous legs.

14

LOOT

ADAM WOKE UP and thought about the slap. Though it hadn't been anywhere near hard enough to leave a mark, it did feel like remnants of Kyle's sausage fingers remained.

Had it been a warning?

Adam didn't know. Perhaps he was reading too much into it, but their terse exchange had come when discussing money, and more importantly, Gerald. Perhaps the slap had been a subliminal message to back off, and to stop all the questioning.

Kyle knew that Adam had done a bit of Sherlocking in the past, he'd alluded to the fact in the interview. Maybe he thought Adam was getting a bit too close for comfort, and was trying to keep him at arm's length, though it wouldn't work. Adam was like a shark with these things. Or if not a shark, at least a tenacious terrier. He couldn't let it go.

And so, he resolved to do something today that, he realised, could get him fired, but he didn't really care. The whole point in taking the job in the first place was to get access to Kyle Baldwin that he wouldn't normally have been able to.

Today was the day to use the free pass to the limit.

After making sure that Helena was still asleep, he got out of bed and, like some sort of crazed hobbit, checked the wedding ring box was still in its hiding place. Thankfully, it was.

He tiptoed out of the bedroom, made some breakfast and then thought a little about what he was planning to accomplish today. He concluded, after running several scenarios, that he'd need to get very lucky.

THE SHOP FLOOR WAS hellish, and Adam was tempted more than once to jack the whole thing in anyway. The stress of two abandoned proposals, coupled with rude customers and the repeated playlist (which hadn't been altered as promised), was really getting to him.

He was about to go and tell Lauren he was quitting when Lady Luck smiled upon him.

At three o'clock, he watched Kyle Baldwin make a beeline for the front door, car keys in hand. Adam assumed that meant he'd be gone for the rest of the day, which in theory meant he could have an uninterrupted snoop in the owner's office. If there was something to be found to link Kyle to Gerald's death, it was either going to be in there or at his home.

As casually as he could, he sloped away from the basket of clothes he was supposed to be hanging up and made his way towards the back. Unfortunately, his route to Kyle's office was blocked by Lauren, who sat at her desk.

'Alright, Adam? How's tricks?' she said.

'All good,' Adam replied. 'How are you?'

'Great, thanks to you. I had a class time with Colin yesterday, so cheers for introducing us.'

'You're grand. Are you seeing each other again?'

'I'd like to, yeah. Things are a bit manic at the moment, but we'll see how it goes.'

'Good to hear,' he smiled. 'Umm… Is Kyle here?'

'He's had to nip out. Did you need him?'

'Ah… Cathy said that there is something wrong with the front door. It's not opening automatically or something. Thought I should tell Kyle.'

'That bleedin' door,' she said, puffing out an indignant sigh. 'I've told him so many times to get it replaced, but he's too much of a skinflint. I'll go down and take a look, see if I need to call someone.'

She got up from behind her desk and Adam followed her out, before peeling off and standing behind a shelf of bathroom items, watching her make her way towards the escalator. When she'd vanished out of sight, he ran to the back.

Kyle had left in such a hurry that he'd not locked his door. Or, perhaps he never did. Adam knew he didn't have much time, so whirred around the office like a careful hurricane. He checked in the filing cabinet and the top of the desk. He rifled through notepads but was met only with order forms, HR reminders and pricing lists.

Lauren was bound to discover she'd been duped at any minute, and Adam gazed around hopelessly, when something jumped out at him.

Kyle's bottom drawer was the only one that had a lock on it, though the key was stuck in it, defeating the point of having a locking drawer entirely. Adam turned the key and found a stack of papers, which he flicked through rapidly. It was mostly more of the same, but two pieces amongst the pile caught his eye.

They'd been shoved in at different places; one near the middle of the stack and one near the bottom.

Both looked like they'd been handled a lot. The corners were dog-eared and uncared for. Adam folded them, shoved them in his pocket and was about to leave the office when he spotted something else.

A notepad on the desk he hadn't seen before. The corner of its pages were poking out from under an A3-sized envelope. He pulled it from its hiding place, and found that the top page had been torn off—remnants of it were caught in the spirals of metal. Whoever had written on it, though, was either in a hurry or angry, as the indentations on the next page down were clear as day.

Meet me tonight.

He took a photo of the page and hurried out onto the shop floor again, where he headed back to his bumper box of clothes, and not a moment too soon. He watched Lauren stride towards the back room, though couldn't see her expression. Hopefully, she'd assume that Adam or Cathy had made a mistake, or that the faulty door had righted itself without the need for intervention.

He kept his head down for the rest of his shift, and when it was time to clock off, texted Colin to ask him to meet in the pub.

It was time to discuss the contents of the pages.

'YOU DID WHAT?!' Adam practically shouted when Colin had finished his story about breaking into Stu Finnegan's house.

'Keep it down,' Colin whispered.

'Why?'

'Because one of his cronies could well be here and listening to you.'

Adam glanced around, and conceded the point. Colin was right. One of Stu's gang of local bandits could be in here, and discussing it at volume was probably a silly thing to do, so Adam lowered his voice but recommenced his tongue-lashing.

'Are you crazy?' he hissed.

'I just thought it would be helpful.'

'You getting yourself killed is pretty far from helpful."

'It's just, it's always you that finds the breakthrough. For once, I wanted to be the one to crack the case.'

'It's not always me that "finds the breakthrough",' Adam said, air quoting the final three words. 'We're a team.'

'I suppose.'

'And I need my best man's head still attached to his body if I ever get the bloody question asked, so promise me that you won't do anything as ridiculously dangerous as that ever again.'

'Scout's honour,' said Colin, holding up a hand with parted fingers.

'That's the Star Trek sign, you numpty!' Adam laughed.

He went to the bar and returned with a couple of drinks. When they'd both taken a few gulps, a corner booth was vacated by a group of lads, so Colin and Adam moved to the relative privacy afforded there.

Adam pulled the pages out and smoothed them on the table. Colin set his pint down and studied what Adam had found.

The scribbles on the first page were written in what looked like fountain pen ink. The paper had been torn from a spiral notebook, and had thin red lines on it. It said:

Jesus. What were you thinking?

The next message was written on a smaller piece of paper, and was tatty and torn in places. The writing was shakier, and looked more childlike. It said:

I'm going to need more. Remember what I know and who I could tell. GA.

'I'm assuming GA is Gerald Agnew,' Colin said.

'I'd say so.'

'So, he sent these to Kyle in the hope of getting more… what?'

'Money, I think, though of course there's no way of being certain.'

'Does it feel like blackmail to you?' Colin asked. 'First, asking Kyle for more money and then threatening him with telling someone something.'

'That's what I thought when I read it.'

'Which means that Kyle might have had something to do with his death? Maybe Kyle went to see Gerald, to pay him to shut up. Maybe things got heated and he ended up killing him by mistake.'

'Or he went to find him to shut him up once and for all, intentionally.'

'What about the first note?' Colin said, pointing to the more legible handwriting.

'They kinda link, I guess. "What were you thinking?"' Adam pointed to the more legible note, and then the scrawled one. '"Remember what I know." Maybe Gerald sent the first one to get Kyle's attention and the second to get him to pay.'

'But the writing is so different?'

'Maybe Gerald got a friend to write one of them so that they couldn't be linked if Kyle got the police involved.'

'What a mess,' Colin sighed. 'You think we should go to the police now?'

'For Whitelaw to tell us that we've been wasting our time and to take the evidence? I don't think so. You and me are going to see this through.'

Colin nodded.

'What's next, then?'

'Well,' Adam said, shoving the phone his way with the picture of the indented notebook on screen. 'Kyle is worried. And when someone is worried, they make mistakes. He's meeting someone tonight, and I think we should be there. Helena is on nights, so I thought we'd head over and stake out Kyle's house. We can follow him to wherever he's going. Maybe he's going to do something crazy.'

'Dude, I know we are finally making progress, but I have an early start at work tomorrow. Do you mind doing this one on your own?'

'No worries,' Adam shrugged. 'I'm sure it'll be a massive waste of time, but you never know.'

They finished their drinks and hit the road; Colin to his warm, comfortable bed and Adam to the confines of his trusty Renault Cleo.

15

YOU CAN TELL A MAN BY HOW HE LIFTS HIS HANDS

ADAM TURNED INTO Kyle Baldwin's street and pulled in between a couple of cars that were parked on the side of the road. It meant he had a clear view of his boss's house, but he was far enough away that he wouldn't be spotted.

He hoped.

The street was in the pricey area of Stonebridge. The houses were detached, the generous gardens well-maintained, and the cars that filled the driveways were a far cry from his own little rust bucket.

He'd swung by the garage before coming here, not knowing how long he'd be keeping a watch on Kyle. He'd hoped that whoever he was meeting was a fan of an early night, and the meeting would be over and done with by the time Match Of The Day started.

The curtains were drawn over Kyle's downstairs windows, though some light filtered out through some gaps in the fabric. Once or twice, a shadow flitted behind the glass, and Adam reckoned Kyle was alone. Perhaps he was getting ready, or summoning up the courage to go to his meeting.

While he sat watching the house, Adam wondered who he could be meeting with. Surely, if Kyle was behind Gerald's demise (and Adam was convinced he was), who could possibly want to share the news with? If that's what he was doing. Maybe he thought the net was closing in on him; perhaps Adam's questions the other night had riled him and he was finding some way to negate his guilt. Maybe he was looking for a scapegoat.

Maybe someone else had ordered Gerald's killing and Kyle was simply a pawn. He doubted it, but he didn't know what to think.

Instead of running endless possibilities around his brain, his thoughts drifted to Colin and the stupidity he'd shown in breaking into Stu's house.

Colin was the one with the managerial role, the one who usually made the sensible choices. Adam wondered what was going on with him at the minute. Was he lonely? Was he trying to prove something by going on a daring, and illegal, mission without having discussed it with Adam first?

Adam reflected on his own behaviour. Since he'd been with Helena, he and Colin had remained close, whilst seeing less of each other. Maybe Adam was partly to blame for his friend's recklessness.

He resolved to make more time for Colin, outside of the cases they undertook. With any luck, this would be their last anyway, and they could simply spend time in the pub or with PlayStation controllers lodged in their hands, trading insults about each other's' FIFA prowess.

Adam's reveries were broken by a car passing by. He ducked down, not knowing why, and watched as the black Honda Jazz came to a stop outside Kyle's house. It idled for a while, before the engine cut and someone got out.

Adam was surprised to see that it was Lauren. As Kyle's PA, he assumed her role was confined to the 9-5 of working hours. Maybe her position called for late night brainstorming meetings, or maybe Adam had simply watched too much The Thick Of It.

What could the boss and his PA possibly have to meet up about?

Was it her that he gave the note to? And if so, why wouldn't he just tell her face to face. It wasn't like they didn't see each other during the day.

Was Lauren somehow linked to Gerald's death?

All of these questions were answered by what happened in the next minute. Adam watched her walk up the drive and ring the bell. She pulled her coat tightly around her and attempted to shelter from the howling wind.

Twenty seconds later, the door opened and Kyle appeared, wearing a white shirt and holding a bottle of wine by the neck. With his spare arm, he pulled her into a tight embrace that ended with a kiss.

And not a friendly kiss on the cheek. This was more akin to the climactic scene from a romcom, where the guy finally gets the girl and has a lot of pent up testosterone to share. Adam could feel the frisson of passion from his cold car.

He also felt the icy knife slip between his shoulder blades as Kyle's front door closed and the realisation hit that he was going to have to break it to Colin that his prospective new girlfriend was two-timing.

He was annoyed.

He thought that tonight would help wrap up, or at least push along, their investigation. But all he was being privy to was a hook-up between a boss and his closest employee.

He considered firing up the engine and going home, but thought that maybe she'd leave soon and he didn't want to miss what happened next, if anything did.

He resolved to stay a little while longer, and then made the mistake of closing his eyes.

THE EARLY MORNING sun made his eyes water and, when he finally managed to open them, he found that it wasn't only his eyes that were sore.

His whole body was in pain.

He'd somehow slept through the night in a cramped, cold car, and every muscle, ligament and tendon was letting him know. He opened the door and straightened his legs, while lying back on the passenger seat to really feel the burn.

His bladder was uncomfortably full and he had no sooner fired up his engine to head home, than Kyle's front door opened.

He killed his motor quickly and watched Lauren dash to her car and take off. Kyle stood and watched her go, leaning casually against the doorframe, before disappearing inside again.

Adam hadn't slept in a car all night to simply walk away from this nonsense.

He got out, locked the door and walked up Kyle's driveway. He pressed the bell, and heard footsteps from inside.

'Forgotten something?' Kyle asked, and then blanched when he saw who was standing in front of him.

'No, but I could do with a wee if you don't mind,' Adam said, pushing in past his trousers-less boss. Whatever was about to happen, one thing was certain—he was definitely losing his job, so he figured he could be as much of a prat as he wanted.

He walked upstairs and found the bathroom. For a single— or at least unmarried—man, the bathroom was surprisingly clean. The taps sparkled and the sink's porcelain shone. Adam did his business and then headed downstairs, finding Kyle in the living room, collapsed on the sofa. Thankfully, he'd found a pair of shorts from somewhere.

'Your PA? Seriously, dude. She's like half your age.'

'You won't tell anyone, will you?' Kyle whimpered.

'Well, considering she and my best friend have been on a date, I might just have to. Be honest with me, and we might be able to keep it between the three of us.'

'I'd appreciate that, you know…'

Adam cut him off by holding his hand up. He needed silence to think.

How he broached this could make or break the case. He decided to start casually.

'How long have you and Lauren been seeing each other?'

'Only for a few weeks. It's nothing serious, but if it gets out, I'll be in big trouble.'

'It doesn't look good, does it? A young, attractive girl in a relationship with the boss man. Some disgruntled employees might be worried about favouritism.'

'That's why it can't get out.'

Adam imagined the Baldwin business empire was flashing before Kyle's eyes. Adam pulled the two pieces of paper from his pocket and laid them on the sofa beside him. He picked one up, the one that said: "I'm going to need more. Remember what I know and who I could tell. GA."

'Tell me about this,' he said.

'Where did you…? Have you been…?'

'Yes, I've been through your office, but let me remind you that I'm the one asking the questions here. You give me an answer I don't like, and the police will be here before you know it.' Adam wafted the piece of paper. 'Tell me about this.'

Any fight left in Kyle Baldwin drifted out of him like a sad ghost. His shoulders slumped and his bottom lip jutted out.

'It's from Gerald, as you have probably guessed. He came in to talk about the Santa gig and saw Lauren and I… you know, on the table. He backed out, respectfully, and then came back the next day and threatened to go to the papers if I didn't give him some money.'

'And did you?'

'The amount he was asking for was a pittance, so I did. A few days later, he came back, asking for more. Out of principle, I said no. I told him that this little act could go on indefinitely, and where to go. His note arrived not long after.'

'So, what did you do?'

'I ignored it. I wasn't going to be bullied by Gerald bloody Agnew. I deal with bigger tossers than him on a daily basis, and I wasn't about to be blackmailed further by that lowlife.'

'And he went away?'

'No. he came back, in person, and had another word. Lauren got a little angry at him, which made him smile. He said some chauvinistic things to her, told me to cough up, and then left.'

'And then you killed him?'

'What?' Kyle actually had the good grace to look shocked. 'Kill him? Of course not.'

'What's this one about then?' Adam asked, holding up the other page. 'It feels vaguely incriminating.'

Jesus. What were you thinking?

'I wrote that one,' Kyle said, shaking his head. 'I realise now how stupid it was to put it down on paper, but at the time it made sense. It was either that or scream until my voice gave out.'

'What does it mean?'

'It was a note to Lauren. But I never gave it to her. I wrote it, and then filed it away.'

'And what *was* she thinking?' Adam asked.

'I don't know. But I'm telling the truth when I say it wasn't me that killed Gerald. It was her.'

'Bull!'

'I swear it. She came to me after she'd done it, in a blind panic. I told her to act like nothing had happened, and it would blow over.'

'What dreadful advice,' Adam laughed.

16

COLOUR THE MESS

BY TEN O'CLOCK, Colin was already clock watching.

Usually, he loved his work, but he knew at the end of today's shift, four long days of holiday were due to begin.

He was feeling burnt out. The endless Christmas songs, the long working hours, the investigation, the smouldering buzz of a potential new relationship. It was all getting on top of him.

Actually, that wasn't fair. The burgeoning relationship was one of the only things keeping him going at the minute, and his mind kept drifting to lovely Lauren as he went about his routine.

'You've got a spring in your step this morning, son,' Barry said. He was wearing a Santa hat and had the beginnings of a beard on his usually clean-shaven face.

'And you look like a hobo,' Colin laughed.

'I'm trying something new. Ladies love a bit of rough,' he said, scratching at the stubble.

'And who do you have your eye on?'

Barry glanced around. 'I'm thinking of inviting Doris for a wee dram on Christmas eve.'

'Doris? Wow. I didn't see that coming. I thought you said she talked too much.'

'Aye, she does a bit. But she's got all the good gossip. Helps pass the day in here.'

Colin had a massive soft spot for Barry, and was pleased that the old man was taking a gamble.

'Well, I'm sure she'll say yes to a wonderful gentleman.'

'A gentleman, probably, but what about me?' Barry chuckled.

Colin wished him luck, and told him to keep him in the loop. Barry walked away and settled in his favourite chair in front of the TV. Doris was nearby, doing some knitting and deep in conversation with Nancy. Colin would have liked to stay and watch, but he had things to do.

Once the retirement home was cleaned, he walked upstairs to the staff room to check his phone. He had a message from Lauren, asking him if he'd like to meet for lunch. He replied that he would, without trying to sound too excited.

He also had twelve missed calls from Adam, which was alarming. He supposed that Adam was ringing to brag that he'd been right all along, and that Kyle Baldwin was currently in a jail cell or in questioning.

Reluctantly, he called Adam back, who answered before the phone could even ring.

'Where have you been?' Adam asked.

'Working. I told you I was in early. What's up?'

Adam launched into the story of the past fourteen hours. Colin's heart sank when he heard about the kiss, and then sank further when he was told that Kyle was currently in police custody, but not for the murder. That, in fact, it was Colin's new flame that had been behind Gerald Agnew's death.

As hard as it was to hear, Colin thanked his friend. Only a true mate would be so honest, and though it hurt, Colin was glad he was finding out now. It wouldn't have done well to take a murderer back to meet the parents.

'She's just texted me, asking to meet for lunch. I'm assuming she hasn't realised that she's been rumbled, and I also assume the police will be looking for her.'

'I'd say so. You should call Whitelaw.'

'I should. Though maybe we can get to her before they do. Take the glory.'

'That's my boy!' Adam whooped.

COLIN AND LAUREN had arranged to meet at a café in the town centre, which told Colin that she was completely oblivious to Adam having rumbled her big secret.

The Town Street Fryer was quiet. It seemed everyone in the town was taking part in a shopping frenzy, abandoning their appetites for fear of missing out on the last action figure or Furby.

Maybe Colin's imagination was simply dredging up memories of watching *Jingle All The Way*.

As it was, they had the place more of less to themselves.

The smell of cooking bacon filled the air. Condensation frosted the front window, cutting off any view of outside. It had started to snow as Colin had parked his car, and he hoped the weather wouldn't stop his guests getting there.

One had already arrived.

Lauren was sitting opposite him, holding his hand across the table. He was trying to act as normally as possible, but was obviously finding it difficult as she kept asking what was wrong. He palmed it off as end of year tiredness, and it looked like she was buying it.

She told him about her night last night. How she'd gone round to her friend's house (Kiera, apparently) and they ended up watching a Christmas film and having a sleepover.

'What did you watch?' Colin asked.

'Love, Actually.'

'I've never seen it.'

'What?' She seemed genuinely shocked. 'That's ridiculous! We should watch it. How about tonight?'

'I can't tonight.'

'Oh. Tomorrow?'

'Let's cut the crap,' Colin whispered, unable to keep up the façade. 'I know about what you did. I know you are seeing Kyle and I know you killed Gerald.'

'What?' she laughed.

'I know,' Colin nodded. 'Adam watched you go into Kyle's house last night and leave this morning. He talked to Kyle, who told him the same story he is probably telling to the police right now.'

'Colin, I'm sorry…'

'Why didn't you just say no when Adam asked if you were single?'

'I thought it would be a good cover. If everyone thought I had a boyfriend, no one would suspect I was with Kyle. People were starting to talk at work, rumours were flying around.'

'Jesus. You've been using me to cover your own arse, and on top of that, you're a bloody murderer.'

'It was an accident,' she shrieked.

The banging and crashing from the kitchen went quiet and one of the chefs' heads appeared through the small serving hole. Colin gave him the thumbs up and he disappeared again.

'It was an accident,' Lauren repeated, quieter this time. 'He was trying to blackmail Kyle. He walked in on us once, and thought he could lord it over us. Kyle and me weren't serious, but the thought of my mum and dad finding out scared me. They wouldn't understand. So, I went and tried to talk to Gerald.'

'And it didn't go well.'

'I tried to talk some sense into him. Told him that the money Kyle was giving him was enough to make a change to his life, and that greediness would get him nowhere. He tried to intimidate me, then. Told me where to get off to. I was about to leave, and he told me that he could give me what Kyle is giving me and more.'

Lauren was crying now.

'He blocked my way out of the alley, and I was scared. It was snowy, and he was that drunk he kept slipping over. The last time he fell, he fell onto his knees. Right near the pole. I grabbed him by the hair and smacked his face into it. I thought it would daze him, give me some time to get away. But I knew from the way he fell I'd hit him too hard.'

'And Kyle covered for you?'

'I told him about it, and he said that it would probably look like an accident. Drunken old fool on slips on a cold night and bangs his head, you know?'

'And then we started looking into it.'

She nods. 'I thought if I could get pally with you, you wouldn't suspect me.'

The door opened at that point, and a set of heavy footsteps sounded on the cheap linoleum flooring. They stopped when they got to Colin's table, and DI Whitelaw slipped into the seat beside him.

'She's all yours,' Colin said, and walked out of the café without a backwards glance.

17

ALIGN THE PLANETS

ADAM AND HELENA clinked their glasses and saluted the incoming new year. They'd eschewed the heaving nightclubs and overpriced taxis and settled for a nice meal at their favourite restaurant and Jools Holland.

They'd got dressed up in their finery, though Adam wished he'd chosen something with a little give in the waist department. The burger and chips had been enough, but he could never resist the honeycomb cheesecake when he came here.

Which was weekly.

As the crooner in the cheap three-piece suit began to murder Sinatra, Adam paid the bill and they left. His hands were sweaty on the steering wheel and when he pulled into their parking space, the butterflies were beating their wings in a frenzy inside his stomach.

'You okay?' Helena asked.

'All good. Just full,' he nodded.

'Tell me about it,' she said, patting her stomach.

They got out, Adam making sure to walk ahead. He led her up the stairs to their flat and put the key in the lock, hoping Colin had been able to put their plan into action.

He turned the key, pushed the door open and heard Helena gasp behind him.

Colin, as ever, had come through.

Every surface of the living room, aside from the flammable ones, had been covered with tealights. Their little flames danced in the draught from the open door. Rose petals formed a sort of red carpet, that led Adam and Helena to a small table, where a bottle of champagne rested in a cooler and two flute glasses awaited. Imogen Heap's Speeding Cars was playing gently on the wireless speaker Adam had got for Christmas.

'What's all this?' Helena asked.

Adam sucked in a deep breath, trying to keep the emotion at bay. He faced her and took her hands in his. He managed to get through most of the speech he'd prepared, though his voice cracked near the end and instead of trying to finish it, he simply got down on one knee and took the ring out of his pocket.

Helena's hand sprung to her mouth as tears began to form in the corners of her eyes.

'Helena Bryer, will you marry me?' he asked.

He knew that he'd remember the small nod of her head and the tight embrace they'd shared after he'd slipped the ring on her finger for the rest of his life.

18

BE A PHOENIX

COLIN SMILED FOR the first time in what felt like days.

Aside from lighting what felt like a million little candles in Adam's house, he'd spent a lonely New Year's in his own home. He hadn't even bothered waiting up to see the new year in.

Hearing Adam gush down the phone that he was engaged, and how impressed Helena had been with the state of the flat, had brightened his outlook somewhat, and as he hung up, he resolved to banish the blues and change his outlook.

Now, he found himself back at work.

'Be a phoenix, son' Barry said. 'It's the first day of a new year and you need to forget that you were courting a murderer. Arise from the ashes, young man, and good things will come.'

'Like you did?'

'Aye, well, I bottled out of asking Doris for a drink, but if you stop moping, maybe I'll get round to it.'

'Deal,' Colin laughed.

He looked around the room.

'Oi, Doris,' he shouted. The old lady looked over the top of her magazine. 'Barry here fancies you and wants to know if you want a drink.'

Barry slapped Colin's leg with a rolled-up newspaper, before looking at Doris expectantly.

'I'd be delighted. Your place or mine?' she laughed, before going back to her photos of the latest celeb to get married.

'Easy as that,' Barry shrugged, and Colin laughed.

He left the lovebirds to it and headed for reception. A new resident was moving in today, and as manager, he wanted to be there to welcome them.

They arrived a short while later. Ken walked in with the aid of a walking stick, and surveyed his surroundings. Colin had met him on a few of the pre-visits, and shook his hand warmly. His family fussed over him, though something in Ken's eyes convinced Colin that he was ready for his next adventure.

Colin walked with him to his room, where they got to know each other for a little while. His daughter and two sons brought a few suitcases and personal belongings in, and Colin was about to leave them to it when a girl popped her head around the door that stopped him in his tracks.

Her long hair was the colour of a tropical beach, and her eyes the colour of the sea that washed upon it. She smiled at Colin, who heard Barry's words reverberate around his head.

'Be a phoenix, son.'

AUTHOR'S NOTE

I love Christmas, so Mistletoe and Crime was a fun one for me to write. I hope you enjoyed it too, and that it got you in the festive spirit! If you got it as a gift, give your friend or family member a big hug from me!

Chapter 4 – The Smiles – may be my favourite chapter I've ever written. All the bands that played in that bar are real, and have long split up. As a teenager, I lived for the local music scene around the north coast of Northern Ireland. I spent most weekends in dive bars, with my friends, listening to bands I loved and having a laugh. Writing this chapter took me right back—to Portrush, to Ballintoy, to band practice at my friend Stephen's house (where we'd play a couple of songs and then resort to football instead, much to Steve's chagrin) and to Exodus (a Christian music venue where my band once played Paranoid by Black Sabbath). It also made me dig out old CDs and get in touch with people I hadn't spoken to in a while, which was lovely. We reminisced and promised to keep in touch more.

Music is powerful, and so are words. I can't thank you all enough for the support you've given me over the past two years(!). Here's to the world opening up bit by bit, and hopefully meeting in the flesh sometime soon.

Cheers!

Chris, November 2021

ABOUT THE AUTHOR

Originally hailing from the north coast of Northern Ireland and now residing in South Manchester, Chris McDonald has always been a reader. At primary school, The Hardy Boys inspired his love of adventure, before his reading world was opened up by Chuck Palahniuk and the gritty world of crime.

He's a fan of 5-a-side football, has an eclectic taste in music ranging from Damien Rice to Slayer and loves dogs.

CPSIA information can be obtained
at www.ICGtesting.com
Printed in the USA
BVHW080858071221
623426BV00005B/218